D0141788

A SPECTER
IS HAUNTING
EUROPE

A
||| SPECTER |||
IS HAUNTING
||| EUROPE |||

A
Sociohistorical
Approach to the
Fantastic

by
José B. Monleón

PRINCETON UNIVERSITY PRESS

PRINCETON, NEW JERSEY

Copyright © 1990 by Princeton University Press
Published by Princeton University Press, 41 William Street,
Princeton, New Jersey 08540
In the United Kingdom: Princeton University Press, Oxford

All Rights Reserved

Library of Congress Cataloging-in-Publication Data
Monleón, José B., 1950–
A specter is haunting Europe : a sociohistorical approach
to the fantastic / José B. Monleón.
p. cm.
Includes bibliographical references.
ISBN 0-691-06862-3 (alk. paper)
1. Fantastic literature, European—History and criticism.
2. Fantastic literature, Spanish—History and criticism.   I. Title.
PN56.F34M59 1990
809.3'8766—dc20   90-33843

This book has been composed in Galliard

Princeton University Press books are printed on acid-free paper,
and meet the guidelines for permanence and durability of the
Committee on Production Guidelines for Book Longevity
of the Council on Library Resources

Printed in the United States of America by
Princeton University Press, Princeton, New Jersey

1 3 5 7 9 10 8 6 4 2

||I CONTENTS I|||

CONTENTS

vi

||■ PREFACE ■|||

THE FANTASTIC has become, without any doubt, a central component of our literary tradition and an increasingly "popular" genre. In our contemporary world of faith in science and technology, it has a wide reading and viewing audience and has invaded movie theaters and the supermarket paperback racks as well as academia. In fact, the fantastic belongs to mass culture and feeds the universe of artistic consumption. It is, at the same time, a primary element in the works of many "recognized" authors: from Hoffmann, Poe, and Maupassant to Borges, García Márquez, and Stephen King, Western literary history incorporates a long tradition of the fantastic, a tradition that encompasses medieval stories as well as modern works, exotic tales from the Orient as well as novels immersed in our mundane, daily life. In the last several decades, the fantastic increasingly has attracted scholarly attention, from various critical perspectives. Psychoanalytic, structuralist, and feminist interpretations—among others—have contributed to a better understanding of this unique form of artistic expression. The present study aims to establish an ideological reading rooted in the concrete historical circumstances from which the fantastic emerged and evolved.

Given the immense number of texts and contexts to be considered, the project required self-imposed limitations. With the exception of Poe, I have considered only the European production; this was done exclusively for historical reasons. This book is thus an introduction in the strictest sense of the word: it sketches, it outlines, it offers a paradigm. In so doing, it makes use of those texts that best serve its purpose—but this purpose, of course, was an a posteriori choice. In this sense I could, and should, endorse Erich Auerbach's comment regarding his study of mimesis: "My interpretations are no doubt guided by a specific purpose. Yet this purpose assumed form only as I went along, playing as it were with my texts, and for long stretches of my way I have been guided only by the texts themselves. Furthermore, the great majority of the texts were chosen at random, on the basis of accidental acquaintance and personal preference rather than in view of a definite purpose" (556). Obviously, many pertinent literary works have not been included—occasionally because they would have required extensive elaboration of subtleties and nuances. Outlines must bear that stigma. They pay a poor tribute to the original text; their simplifications can never do justice to the rich intricacies of a single story. Yet it is also true that part of that individual richness is due to the recognition that a text shares some elements with other individual texts. Texts create paradigms and paradigms create texts. *Don Quixote* shapes the idea of the novel as much as the novel shapes *Don Quixote*. This is part of the process of literary evolution. Therefore, departures from the model do not necessarily negate the model. On the contrary, they enhance it through modification, as I know further studies of the fantastic will enhance this one.

The present book is, then, as the title indicates, an introduction to the social history of the fantastic. It intends to frame, both in space and in time, the basic conditions that produced and were reproduced by what we now understand, very loosely, as the fantastic. In it I have used the works and ideas of numerous critics and historians who do not always concur ideologically or methodologically. The names of Todorov, Foucault, Lukács, Hobsbawm, and Himmelfarb seem at odds under the same roof. The book is neither an effort at critical pluralism nor an attempt to establish a synthesis of different and opposing currents. I have "expropriated" those findings that I considered correct and useful in the construction of the present study, regardless of whether or not I agreed with the general ideas or conclusions of each author. I am neither applying a particular method nor following a specific school of criticism, although I am sure that the reader will be able to discern the perspective from which the issues are approached.

The book consists of three main parts: chapter 1 is a discussion of the fantastic in theoretical terms; chapters 2, 3, and 4 are concerned with the fantastic in industrially advanced countries such as England, France, and the United States. The chapters follow an evolutionary line, with each one concerned with the characteristics and problems of the fantastic in a given period. This periodization does not imply the successive rise and fall of certain types of the fantastic. It indicates that during a certain span of time a particular kind of the fantastic came into being and was predominant, but it does not exclude the possibility that previous forms subsisted in later stages.

Chapter 5 is likewise an introduction, but it focuses on the Spanish production. Many of its theses must be regarded as hypotheses rather than definite conclusions, since a general vacuum envelops the Spanish fantastic. Nevertheless, the section is necessary and useful insofar as it serves not only to introduce the Peninsular phenomenon but also to verify the European paradigm. Spain's late development, as well as its economic and cultural dependence, offers a distinct background against which to test the flexibility and reliability of the previous findings. Germany or Russia could have served equally as a concrete example on which to test the model.

Finally, a word about some formal aspects. Bibliographical information about works cited is provided in the bibliography at the end of the book. In the text, numbers in parentheses indicate the page number (and, if necessary for clarification, the date) of the work cited. As for translations, they are mine, except where otherwise indicated.

A SPECTER
IS HAUNTING
EUROPE

ⅢⅡ ONE ⅢⅡ

Introduction

1

Tzvetan Todorov's *The Fantastic* has become an unavoidable cornerstone of any attempt to analyze fantastic literature. It represents a concerted effort to mark the boundaries and identify the characteristics, from a structuralist perspective, of this literary genre. It seems appropriate, then, to begin with Todorov's definition of the fantastic:

> In a world which is indeed our world, the one we know, a world without devils, sylphides, or vampires, there occurs an event which cannot be explained by the laws of this same familiar world. The person who experiences the event must opt for one of two possible solutions: either he is the victim of an illusion of the senses, of a product of the imagination—and laws of the world then remain what they are; or else the event has indeed taken place, it is an integral part of reality—but then this reality is controlled by laws unknown to us. . . . The fantastic occupies the duration of this uncertainty. Once we choose one answer or the other, we leave the fantastic for a neighboring genre, the uncanny or the marvelous. The fantastic is that hesitation experienced by a person who knows only the laws of nature, confronting an apparently supernatural event. (25)

The basic concept that must be taken into consideration, according to Todorov, is uncertainty. The fantastic in literature evolves around a doubt in the interpretation of the nature of the events presented in the narration. The fantastic as a literary genre, then, must be approached as an epistemological problem. From this initial proposition Todorov goes on to identify the three basic conditions of the fantastic: "First, the text must oblige the reader to consider the world of the characters as a world of living persons and to hesitate between a natural and a supernatural explanation of the events described. Second, this hesitation may also be experienced by a character. . . . Third, the reader must adopt a certain attitude with regard to the text: he will reject allegorical as well as 'poetic' interpretations" (33). The first and third conditions are necessary in order to enter the realm of the fantastic; the second one may or may not occur. Hence the weight of the definition resides in the reader—a conclusion that must necessarily create tension with the underlying structuralist premises of the book. Todorov solves the conflict by resorting to the concept of the implicit reader in the text. Yet such a formalization of the problem does not adequately address the initial epistemological proposition, since surely the characteristics of such an implicit reader would depend on the historical determinants that framed the text. Thus, when considering the *Arabian Nights*, Todorov claims that "supernatural events are reported without being presented as such. The implicit reader is supposed to be ignorant of the region where the events take place, and consequently he has no reason for calling them into question. . . . The mixture [of natural and supernatural elements] exists, of course, only for the modern reader; the narrator implicit in the tale situates everything on the same level (that of the 'natural')" (55–56). The *Arabian Nights* would thus fall under the category of the marvelous, a genre closely linked to the fantastic and characterized by the presentation of supernatural events without any acknowledgment of a "hesitation." But, as Todorov himself points out, such supernatural elements can be entertained as such only by a modern reader. Why, then, should it be considered a "marvelous" work? If the narrator in the tale situates everything on the natural level, should the story not be considered "mimetic" or "realistic," in the broader sense of the term?[1] "In a world which is indeed our world," says Todorov, "there occurs an event which cannot be explained by the laws of this same familiar world." But what must we understand by the

4

laws of our world? Should a story written in the Middle Ages be considered according to the concept of nature upheld in those times or according to our current understanding of reality? Should the genre of a work change as the history of humanity modifies the idea of nature?

This apparently elusive character of the fantastic becomes for Louis Vax its basic defining trait. After rejecting the idea that nature should be taken into consideration,[2] he concludes that the fantastic cannot be apprehended through understanding or judgment but is rather perceived by the senses, like the "tragic or comic modes." "We laugh," he says, "because the comic aspects of a situation strike us *naturally*, and not because thinking shows us the superimposition of mechanical elements over live elements" (18; emphasis mine). The tautology is clear: starting from a negation of the natural, given its polysemous character, he ends by accepting the fantastic as a natural component of our sensibility. For Vax, then, the fantastic is an ingredient of human nature, an empirical phenomenon apprehended without mediation, while for Todorov it is, ultimately, an epistemological question, although he does not pursue the implications of such premises to their final historical conclusions. Fantastic literature, according to Vax, encompasses an aspect of the entire history of artistic production. Todorov, in contrast, in using selected texts from the eighteenth and nineteenth centuries, *implicitly* limits the fantastic to that period.[3]

A consensus seems to exist in dating the origins of the Gothic tale, and of fantastic narrative in general, to 1764, with the publication of Horace Walpole's *The Castle of Otranto*.[4] Sir Walter Scott, in his introduction to one of the consecutive reprints, presented one of the first analyses of this new genre: "In *The Castle of Otranto*, it was his [Walpole's] object to unite the marvellous turn of incident, and imposing tone of chivalry, exhibited in the ancient romance, with that accurate exhibition of human character, and contrast of feelings and passions, which is, or ought to be, delineated in the modern novel" (6). "It was his object to draw such a picture of domestic life and manners,

5

during the feudal times, as might actually have existed, and to paint it chequered and agitated by the action of supernatural machinery, such as the superstition of the period received as matter of devout credulity. The natural parts of the narrative are so contrived, that they associate themselves with the marvellous occurrences; and by the force of that association, render those *speciosa miracula* striking and impressive, though our cooler reason admits their impossibility" (8). Scott acknowledges the coexistence in this "new kind of narrative," as he calls it, of two epistemological systems that belong to different historical periods: one corresponding to the "unreasonable" world of the Middle Ages, and another related to "more enlightened ages," to a society in which the principles of reason appear to shape nature. It is this coexistence, as articulated through the blending of the romance and the modern novel, that accounts for the labeling of *Otranto* as a new narrative. The fact that Walpole introduces supernatural events is not the important factor. What matters is the *association*, within the realm of artistic representation, of those "speciosa miracula" with the elements of the modern novel. The Gothic was born out of the interaction, in one space, of two opposed and irreconcilable worldviews; it came into being as the result of the tensions produced by the inclusion of medieval beliefs within the reasonable framework of eighteenth-century bourgeois precepts. The Gothic was, therefore, an artistic antinomy, a paradox at the level of representation that challenged the principles of modern art and, therefore, of modern society. The fantastic was thus born, and from this moment its history and characteristics would be determined by the constant shifting of the diffuse boundaries between reason and unreason.[5]

Clearly Scott's definition implies that fantastic literature, from the perspective of the postclassical period, could not have existed before its emergence at the end of the 1700s. Scott based his arguments on a sense of historical development, of progress, since the nature of some events, although "held impossible by more enlightened ages, was yet consonant with the faith of earlier times" (10). This initial appraisal of fantastic literature has not been generally accepted by more modern critics—as the cases of Todorov and Vax illustrate. And yet it is precisely by assuming the historical connotations of such a genre, as did Scott, that a more comprehensive study of the fantastic can be undertaken. From the outset, however, a distinction must be made between the fantastic and fantasy, that is, between a literary genre and a human attribute. For if such a distinction were not established, the totality of artistic production would have to be considered in these pages, and an entirely different problem would be at issue. Yet the question of "fantasy and mimesis" is, to a certain extent, relevant to the study of the fantastic, at least insofar as it addresses a particular conception of reality. If the fantastic, as I argue, depends deeply on a specific concept of reality, of what is true and natural, then surely there must be a literature, prior to *Otranto*, that deals with this issue, even if the referential premises rest on different values.

This is, to a point, true. Kathryn Hume proposes that "literature is the product of two impulses. These are *mimesis*, felt as the desire to imitate . . . and fantasy, the desire to change givens and alter reality" (20). The basic question, nevertheless, is not solved by such a definition. What is to be imitated? What reality is to be changed? Any answer would have to take into account different historical and cultural worldviews: "We can also include as fantasy those stories whose marvel is considered 'real', although not in the same fashion that a chair is real. Miracles and some monsters may have been thought to exist by their original audience and even their author, but were often acknowledged to be real only in a special fashion: they only enter the lives of the spiritually or heroically elect; they are *miracula* or things to be marvelled at, precisely because they are not everyday occurrences and cannot be controlled by just anybody who has a mind to try" (Hume, 21). Fantasy, from this perspective, would be uncommon reality, an exotic experience—but reality nonetheless. The fact that it was experienced

7

only by a select group precludes neither its existence nor its effects on society at large. The Spanish poet Gonzalo de Berceo, for instance, wrote during the thirteenth century hagiographies of local saints and recorded the miracles performed by the Virgin, creating texts that were later used as legal documents by the Monastery of San Millán in order to claim economic gains. The miracles of Our Lady were indeed miracula, but they fell within the realm of absolute reality.

In a more illuminating passage Hume states that "Christian fantasy encouraged the non-real, but did not sharpen critical awareness of the phenomenon because fantasy, if it served the cause of morality, became 'true' and therefore ethically distinct from the lies of fable" (7). Assuming that by "non-real" Hume means uncommon reality, as she herself indicates, truth, and thus reality, were determined on moral grounds. Nature responded to the desires and designs of God, as interpreted by the church. Therefore, unnatural events could reside only in the domain of lies. Miracula might exist, the supernatural might be recognized; but whether these were the product of fantasy or of reality, of imagination or of mimesis, depended upon ethical and political dictates. Under these conditions, it is impossible to talk about the fantastic, since this implies the recognition of the supernatural not on moral grounds but, paradoxically, on rational premises. Not until nature became objectified, and not until the supernatural was equated with the unnatural, could fantastic literature emerge. For Rosemary Jackson, "the issue of the narrative's internal reality is always relevant to the fantastic, with the result that the 'real' is a notion which is under constant interrogation" (36). Prior to the triumph of reason, a work meeting these criteria would have been considered heretic, not fantastic.

The fantastic is not, therefore, fantasy. In fact, there must first exist a world like "our world, the one we know without devils, sylphides, or vampires" before this genre can appear: "The literature of the occult operates in that area where these two worlds clash head on—that sense of radical disjunction, that thrill, the sensation of numbing dislocation which arises at that point of intersection between two separate worlds, the material and the supernatural. It is this sense of *fracture* which provides the real power of this type of literature" (Messent, 2). For this fracture to take place, an exclusive worldview—one that recognizes the existence of nature as ruled by independent laws that cannot be transgressed—needs first to dominate in society. The fantastic is, at heart, an epistemological question, not an ethical one, although it does have profound philosophical and political consequences, as I will delineate in the following pages. This is why, as Todorov indicates, allegory and poetry (at least nonnarrative poetry) cannot be considered part of the fantastic expression: "If as we read a text we reject all representation, considering each sentence as a pure semantic combination, the fantastic *could not appear*: for the fantastic requires, it will be recalled, a reaction to events as they occur in the world evoked. For this reason, the fantastic can subsist only within fiction; poetry cannot be fantastic" (60). "If what we read describes a supernatural event, yet we take the words not in their literal meaning but in another sense which refers to nothing supernatural, there is no longer any space in which the fantastic can exist" (63–64). Of course, in all fairness, this assertion would require a more extensive study of allegory, a category in itself that is also far from remaining unchanged in the course of historical development.[6] Such a study, unfortunately, would fall beyond the scope of this work. In principle, however, the premise should be accepted. Undoubtedly some allegorical connotations can be found in books like *Frankenstein* or *Dr. Jekyll and Mr. Hyde*. For Rosemary Jackson, Stevenson's novel "is usually seen as the clearest allegory of Victorian hypocrisy and repression" (114). Yet if one of the basic mechanisms of the fantastic is to question the premises of the natural, then allegory, in the strictest sense of the word, must be discarded. As Sigmund Freud noted in *The Uncanny*: "So long as

9

they remain within their setting of poetic reality, such [supernatural] figures lose any uncanniness which they might possess" (250).

2

Let us return to Scott's introduction to Walpole's *Otranto*: "Romantic narrative is of two kinds—that which, being in itself possible, may be matter of belief at any period; and that which, though held impossible by more enlightened ages, was yet consonant with the faith of earlier times. The subject of *The Castle of Otranto* is of the latter class. Mrs. Radcliffe . . . has endeavoured to effect a compromise between those different styles of narrative, by referring her prodigies to an explanation, founded on natural causes, in the latter chapters of her romances" (10). Scott's classification of "Romantic" narrative[7] establishes the basis for more contemporary evaluations of the fantastic. It relates in particular to Todorov's basic categories: the marvelous (in which supernatural events are accepted without hesitation) and the uncanny (in which plausible events project a shadow of supernaturalism).[8] The fantastic in its purest form, according to Todorov, could barely exist as a genre, since "the fantastic occupies the duration of this uncertainty. Once we choose one answer or the other, we leave the fantastic for a neighboring genre, the uncanny or the marvelous. The fantastic is that hesitation *experienced by a person* who knows only the laws of nature, confronting an apparently supernatural event" (25; emphasis mine). Only texts such as Henry James's *The Turn of the Screw* would then fall under the category of the fantastic.

Moving beyond the fact that the fantastic, as a genre, conspicuously disappears from Todorov's diagram, it seems certain that the central question sustaining each category remains directly attached to the concept of the supernatural. But is this a sufficient condition? As Todorov himself points out, in apparent contradiction to his own implicit premises, "the supernatural, though a literary category, of course, is not relevant here. We cannot conceive a genre which would regroup all works in which the supernatural intervenes and which would thereby have to accommodate Homer as well as Shakespeare, Cervantes as well as Goethe. The supernatural does not characterize works closely enough, its extension is much too great" (34). This last remark is certainly true. Yet, if not sufficient, the supernatural must at least be a necessary condition.

Another often-cited component of the fantastic is fear. Todorov, once again, dismisses it: "If we take their [critics'] declarations literally—that the sentiment of fear must occur in the reader—we should have to conclude that a work's genre depends on the *sang-froid* of its reader. Nor does the determination of the sentiment of fear in the *characters* offer a better opportunity to delimit the genre" (35). A similar argument could be made in relation to the theory of hesitation and the degree of "credulity" of the reader—whether implicit or not. For numerous writers and critics, nevertheless, fear emerges in one way or another as closely linked with the fantastic. In her essay "On the Supernatural in Poetry" Ann Radcliffe had already tied the question of the supernatural to that of fear. She established three categories: terror, horror, and mystery: "Terror suggests the frenzy of physical and mental fear of pain, dismemberment, and death. Horror suggests the perception of something incredibly evil or morally repellent. Mystery suggests something beyond this, the perception of a world that stretches away beyond the range of human intelligence—and thereby productive of a nameless apprehension that may be called religious dread in the face of the wholly other" (Messent, 34). G. R. Thompson examines the same subject, and affirms that fantastic literature would result from a combination of these different types of fear. He goes on to qualify further the differences between terror and horror: "Terror . . . may be seen as coming upon us from without . . . whereas horror rises up from within, with a vague consciousness of the dreader evil sinking downward through levels of subconscious uncertainty and obscurity into a vast unconscious reservoir of primitive dread" (34).

Some inferences can be made from these two series of definitions, set well apart in time. Terror is a response to causes that originate in the natural world and that can be recognized and explained: fear of pain, dismemberment, and so on. Horror belongs to an inexplicable category, since it is an "incredible evil" that arises from a "reservoir of primitive dread." Of course, what separates these two authors in their accounts of horror is the discovery of the unconscious as a tool for understanding and explaining the roots of that internal and otherwise incomprehensible fear. For Radcliffe, horror is still perceived as a moral distinction, akin to the concept of the supernatural in "less enlightened" times, when the unconscious had not yet been objectified and naturalized. Given these premises, an association can be established between the different expressions of fear and Todorov's classifications of the supernatural: terror-uncanny (explained); horror-marvelous (unexplained); mystery-fantastic (the possibility of a different world is suggested but no definite answer is offered). This last category, as might be expected, would persist only as long as no solution in either direction was reached.

Of course, horror today can be deciphered and attributed to natural causes. It can be explained psychologically. But the marvelous as well can be rationalized, as shown, for instance, by the great number of psychological interpretations of Franz Kafka's *The Metamorphosis*. This argument, in any case, is not so much a defense of the fear theory as an attempt to show that a close relation exists between the supernatural and fear in the composition of fantastic literature—although the determination of the exact makeup of this genre or even of the definition of these elements is not, at this point, my objective.

Fear however, like the supernatural, is a very broad category that needs further consideration. According to Freud, "the subject of the 'uncanny' is . . . undoubtedly related to what is frightening—to what arouses dread and horror. . . . Yet we may expect that a special core of feeling is present which justifies the use of a special conceptual term. One is curious to know what this common core is which allows us to distinguish as 'uncanny' certain things which lie within the field of what is frightening" (219). In "The Uncanny" ("Das Unheimlich," 1919) Freud traces the semantic origins of the word to note that *Heimlich* and *Unheimlich* ultimately mean the same thing: the familiar. Unheimlich is not, according to him, a contradictory term but rather denotes a concept that belongs to two different sets of ideas: "On the one hand it means what is familiar and agreeable, and on the other, what is concealed and kept out of sight" (224–25). The paradoxical quality of the term, as I will later argue, points precisely to the basis of the fantastic. For Freud, however, it leads to the idea of repression: the fear embedded in an uncanny experience would be provoked by the "coming into light" of what at one point was familiar and should have remained secret. Why, for instance, does the concept of the double produce uneasiness? "When all is said and done, the quality of uncanniness can only come from the fact of the 'double' being a creation dating back to a very early mental stage, long since surmounted—a stage, incidentally, at which it wore a more friendly aspect. The 'double' has become a thing of terror, just as, after the collapse of their religion, the gods turned into demons" (236). The uncanny then becomes a projection—a dream of sorts—of the canny. They are not disconnected concepts but rather lie on a continuum. Just as for Goya monsters were the product of reason, so too is the Unheimlich the end result of the familiar.

This theory would serve to explain, in general terms, the presence of medieval images and themes in the pages of fantastic literature; it would also account for the predominance of sexual references. Rosemary Jackson makes use of the principles of repression to formulate a sociohistorical analysis of the fantastic. Closely following Freud, she asserts that the uncanny "uncovers what is hidden and, by doing so, effects a disturbing transformation of the familiar into the unfamiliar" (65). Hence

13

the power of this literature would reside in its faculty of representing "that which cannot be said, that which evades articulation" (37). However, such a paradox (the verbalization of the ineffable) is not assumed by Jackson as a central philosophical and ideological question in need of resolution—a resolution that would need to be reached within the framework of historical conflict. Nonetheless, her otherwise interesting study does provide a social context from which to approach the fantastic. Her labeling of the fantastic as a "literature of subversion"[9] responds to an appraisal of fantastic literature as cultural production: "Fantastic literature points to or suggests the basis upon which cultural order rests, for it opens up, for a brief moment, on to disorder, on to illegality, on to that which lies outside the law, that which is outside dominant value systems. The fantastic traces the unsaid and the unseen of culture: that which has been silenced, made invisible, covered over and made 'absent' " (4). But the exposition of the repressed is not necessarily a subversive act, if by subversion is meant a challenge to the causes of repression, a defiance of order, an assault on dominant ideology. As I argue in this book, the fantastic played exactly the opposite role: that is, the defense of the status quo and the preservation of economic order. If anything, it served precisely to help modify hegemonic discourse in order to justify the survival of bourgeois society, a fact that also explains why the fantastic appeared only after the bourgeoisie had consolidated its power.[10] The questioning of order is not necessarily a subversive act. The perspective from which that questioning is undertaken as well as the implicit or explicit alternatives derived from such an action must also be taken into account.

In any case, Jackson's remarks undoubtedly shed some light on a crucial aspect of fantastic literature, one avoided by the critics previously mentioned: its role as ideology. From these premises, the theory of repression can be pursued as a means of clarifying and understanding the fantastic. Tobin Siebers incorporates some of Michel Foucault's notions to emphasize the importance of this concept: "The idea of exclusion serves the critic of fantastic literature particularly well because fantastic stories often reproduce exclusionary gestures. Even at its most superficial level, fantastic literature refers to ideas and characters existing outside of natural laws" (27). Foucault's ideas are certainly important in understanding the dynamics behind the fantastic, and I will draw on his conclusions in the next chapter. But Siebers brings the argument back to the initial discussion, that is, the definition of the characteristics of those natural laws. Siebers embarks upon this task: "The essential literary and historical question to be answered here concerns the nature of the interference among the Romantic, fantastic, and supernatural. Supernaturalism is a difficult issue to discuss, however, especially today when any mention of the word risks casting one's intentions and scholarship in doubt. It is at once the most obvious and most ignored aspect of fantastic literature" (11). Unfortunately, supernaturalism becomes for Siebers superstition, "a logic common to all people, whether non-Western or Western" (12). Thus, in spite of the fact that he sets out to create a historical and literary context that could facilitate the reading of fantastic masterpieces, he introduces a factor, superstition, that is in itself deprived of historical significance, since by definition it is offered as a transcultural (and one must also assume "transclassist") human quality. The shadow of this premise will hover over his analysis of the romantic fantastic.

3

Both Tobin Siebers and Rosemary Jackson have understood the need to incorporate a historical framework in order to comprehend fully the nature and significance of the fantastic. When faced with Todorov's diagram, both scholars sensed that a diachronic outline could be deduced. In the words of Jackson, "Todorov's diagrammatic representation of the changing forms of the fantastic makes this clear: they move from the marvellous (which predominates in a climate of belief in supernaturalism and magic) through the purely fantastic (in which no explanation can be found) to the uncanny (which explains all strangeness as generated by unconscious forces)" (24–25). This movement seems difficult to accept, for it denies, for instance, a place in this vector for Latin American literature, written since the turn of the twentieth century, that conforms to the characteristics of the marvelous—a literature that could hardly be dismissed as non-Western. But even within the European production, and even considering that the assertion refers to dominant tendencies, the proposal is extremely questionable. Jean Pierrot, for instance, defends an opposite evolution: "From the point of view of the history of the imaginary, [the decadent aesthetics] constitutes a capital stage in an evolution that starting from the romantic fantastic ends up in the surrealist marvelous" (19). I adhere more closely to this last suggestion. For, as I will argue, if one considers the modern fantastic—or, more precisely, the fantastic in the age of capitalism—as a radically distinct artistic expression, as a new kind of narrative that cannot be equated with the production of earlier social organizations, then clearly the evolution of this genre follows the opposite direction from the one indicated by Jackson and Siebers. Taking as a basis the epistemological question of uncertainty, it follows a line proceeding, in simplified terms, from the uncanny (in which an answer of some sort, either rational or irrational, is provided) through the "pure" fantastic (in which the question of uncertainty becomes itself the answer) to the marvelous (in which the question in fact disappears from the realm of representation): from Walpole (or Radcliffe) through Poe to Kafka.

Such an evolution, it must be emphasized, does not pretend to be a neatly drawn line with immaculate cells in which to deposit each particular text. On the contrary, it denotes only a general trend and dominant tendencies. Individual works can and must present resistance to the paradigm, defiance of the rules that try to constrain them to a genre or pattern. Otherwise, difference and evolution would not exist. And yet, in order to achieve a generic definition, the task of confronting generalities, with the risks involved in it, must be undertaken: "Definitions acquire their full meanings in the course of a historical process. They cannot be used intelligently unless we humbly concede that their penumbrae are not easily penetrated by linguistic short-cuts. If, through fear of possible misunderstandings, we agree to eliminate the historical elements and to offer supposedly atemporal sentences as definitions, we deny ourselves the intellectual heritage bequeathed to philosophy from the beginning of thought and experience" (Horkheimer, 165). Thus the definition of the fantastic requires a historical approach, since a genre cannot exist outside of elapsed time.[11] And just as the study of a genre demands the study of individual texts and vice versa, if a comprehensive identification of the fantastic is to be formulated two main coordinates must be taken into consideration: first, the changing historical meaning of the fantastic in different periods; and second, the role of the fantastic in determining this meaning, in creating history.[12] For the latter purpose, I have chosen a periodization that, as I have already mentioned, by no means pretends to be absolute. The dates that head each chapter of this book do not represent "epistemes," to use Foucault's terminology, but rather brief periods that can be identified as assuming a transcendental significance insofar as they condense the fundamental forces of the historical development outlined in these pages. As for the characteristics of the fantastic, the defining elements do not belong exclusively to the realm of fantastic literature, and I will often draw from examples not directly related to it but which nonetheless play an important role in clarifying historical meaning. These elements will combine to create an artistic form whose *most appropriate expression* will be called the fantastic. According to Horkheimer, "each concept must be seen as a fragment of an inclusive truth in which it finds its meaning. It is precisely the building of truth out of such fragments that is philosophy's prime concern" (167).

What, then, are these elements, these fragments, of the fan-

17

tastic? Three fundamental components can be extracted from the theories and definitions proposed by the critics mentioned in the preceding pages.[13] The fantastic seems to arise out of:

(1) an epistemological question relating to an uncertainty about or questioning of the nature of some events

(2) a sociopsychological problem that finds an expression through the articulation of fear

(3) an ideological and historical framework in which the fantastic interconnects with other cultural and social currents.

In practice, these three components do not act separately, either in representation or in reality. Hence in the chapters that follow I give an account that avoids extreme artificial compartmentalization and eludes dualistic analysis, by interweaving these elements and inserting them into broader problems. The book is, then, in this sense a social history of the fantastic.

The first element requires an appraisal of the coordinates that delineate the concept of nature, material as well as social, at a given time. It is clear that a correspondence exists in history between the way people envisage the law of the physical world and the way they see the law of society. Thus when supernaturalism finds a voice in cultural production, it may certainly refer to a material as well as a social supernaturalism. A correlation must exist between the defiance of nature and the challenge to society.

The second aspect, fear, has a wide range of manifestations. Besides the categories already mentioned of terror, horror, and the uncanny, many other levels and nuances of fright could be introduced. Fracture and head-on clash, as G. R. Thompson qualifies it, and conflict in general could be related concepts. Siebers, for instance, indicates that "if the evolution of supernaturalism relates to violence, as many social scientists have suggested, then the fantastic, as an aesthetic form of superstition, may also involve patterns of social and interpersonal conflict" (61). Under this broad category of conflict and fear (which should actually be perceived as the two poles, cause and

18

effect, of the same problem), the question that must be addressed relates once again to the nature of these elements' existence, to the role they play in shaping the meaning of the fantastic, to their function as a cultural form. The fantastic would then be an artistic production articulating a social concern about the essence of nature and law, on the one hand, and the threats and fears derived from such a concern, on the other. The fantastic is thus based on antinomy.

This definition is, however, incomplete, for the terms that shape it are still too abstract. In order to attempt a more concrete appraisal, a third element, history, must be included within the defining parameters: "The strategic value of generic concepts for Marxism clearly lies in the mediatory function of the notion of a genre, which allows the coordination of immanent formal analysis of the individual text with the twin diachronic perspective of the history of forms and the evolution of social life" (Jameson, 105). The inclusion of history, therefore, cannot be reduced to an idealist approach, that is, to the presentation of the fantastic within a "history of ideas." Tobin Siebers views his work as "an interdisciplinary study of comparatist scope that tries to establish a context in which to view the little masterpieces of fantastic literature. This context may be called historical, but not in the traditional sense because I am more interested in identifying certain strategies that evolve with regard to literature and superstition than in defining periods. If there is a view of history presented here, it defines historical consciousness as the product of a convergence between the literary imagination and the growing awareness of violence in society" (12–13).

History, historical consciousness, then becomes the result of the combination of imagination and consciousness. Such a self-serving, idealist position negates the role of material conditions in the shaping of consciousness, thus leading to questionable conclusions. Siebers appropriately identifies the relation between reason and irrationality as crucial to understanding the fantastic. Yet by looking at these two concepts outside of material determinants, outside of class conflict, he identifies ideology with reality. According to Siebers, in the eighteenth century the "Rationalists worked to demystify all forms of supernatural representation, religious and magical, because they associated it with the violence of ideological persecution. Their attempt to eradicate such victimization, however, was only partially successful insofar as they maintained an aggressive attitude toward believers in religion and magic" (123). This apparent contradiction on the part of the "Rationalists," presented by Siebers as a kind of ontological duality, can be resolved only if political and economic considerations are taken into account. The principles of reason were laid out in opposition to the dominance of arbitrary absolutism and feudal organization. Once the "Rationalists" were in power, however, a very different political configuration came into being, with the end result that reason had to adjust in order to conform to its new social role. This is precisely the moment at which the fantastic enters the social imagination and begins to help shape social consciousness. But the perspective from which reason exercises its influence must also be acknowledged. When Siebers affirms that "the Romantics in turn identified rational skepticism with insensitivity and violence, and their embrace of the fantastic was at heart a nonviolent and sympathetic gesture toward the outcasts of Reason" (27), he overlooks some important considerations. The romantics—a term in itself in need of further clarification—might have perceived themselves as outcasts, or they might have embraced self-banishment as a means of sympathetically assuming the plight of the repressed. The romantics might have questioned the reasonable society from an aristocratic position, or from a more populist and revolutionary stance. But what seems clear in historical, political, and economic terms is that in the age of capitalist supremacy, since the end of the eighteenth century, the real outcasts were "the laboring and dangerous classes"—and that the main voice these classes adopted was not the cry of unreason, but rather the language of reason.

|||| TWO ||||

1789:
The Dream
of Reason

1

ON FEBRUARY 6, 1799, the *Diario de Madrid* announced—or, more precisely, advertised—the publication of *Los Caprichos*, a series of eighty aquatint plates by Francisco Goya. In retrospect, this date stands out as an epistemological turning point both in the personal evolution of Goya's style and in the development of art history. With *Los Caprichos* the Spanish painter set in motion an artistic production (*The Disasters of War*, *Los Disparates*,[1] *The Black Paintings*, and so on) that made him a forerunner—the father, as Philip Hofer calls him—of modern art. Successive generations, from romantics to surrealists, would appropriate Goya's art and trace a continuity between their own production and Goya's.

According to some preliminary sketches, the series of *Los Caprichos* should have begun with what we now identify as plate 43, "El sueño de la razón produce monstruos" ("The Sleep of Reason Produces Monsters"). Goya's final decision to change the order may have been politically motivated, since this plate bears a strong resemblance to the title page of the 1783 edition of Rousseau's *Philosophie*, a work banned in Spain during the 1790s as dangerously subversive. Whatever the case, it seems certain that this particular *Capricho,* the only one containing a title, assumes a special significance within the series. Conceived as the opening plate, it encapsulates the basic theme of the collection: the artist, leaning on his desk, sleeps; behind him, strange animals occupy the space of darkness. "Fantasy abandoned by reason," reads the legend, "produces impossible

21

monsters; united with reason, fantasy is the mother of the arts and the source of their wonders."[2] As the pages unfold, the reader is confronted by an uncanny world, a monstrous universe of deformity and aberration; the eighty aquatint plates build a space precisely for those impossible monsters to be acknowledged within the realm of art.

In principle, *Capricho 43* seems to condense the postulates of the Enlightenment: where reason fails, the forces of the occult prevail. Thus, the plate is structured around a binary axis contrasting and opposing two grounds. In the foreground is a man clearly delineated, a man brought into our vision by light, a man who has just been writing (an act that the classical age viewed as the absolute domain of reason); in the background, animal-monsters, beasts whose diffused contours melt away in the surrounding darkness, seem to lay siege to the world of reason. Two irreconcilable universes face one another: the kingdom of light and truth on the one side, the anarchy of darkness and error on the other. The ultimate resolution of the battle between reason and unreason is determined well in advance, since the awakening of the leaning man will dissipate the threat of chaos. And yet it is precisely the coexistence of two exclusive systems in one sign, the space of plate 43, that gives Goya's work a different dimension, projecting a new artistic expression. Ernst Gombrich notes in his study of romantic art that "in periods such as the Middle Ages . . . the configuration of images is understood and read as purely symbolic. With the victory of a realistic conception of art, however, a dilemma makes itself felt. To a public, accustomed to see images as representations of a visual reality, the mere juxtaposition of disconnected symbols produces a disquieting paradox in need of resolution" (Licht, 155–56). This uncomfortable paradox will define the core of the fantastic, as well as all or most of post-Enlightenment art, a fact that helps explain the constant reappropriation of Goya by successive artistic movements. In order to understand the construction of this paradox, it is necessary first to trace some of the developments leading to the "victory" of the realistic conception of visual reality.

In the first book of *Don Quixote* (1605), the scrutiny of the protagonist's library can be read as, among other things, a lesson in literary criticism. The priest's criteria for saving or condemning a book are revealing: those books that adhere to a sense of truth or realistic representation, that remain within the boundaries of the *vraisemblable*, will be spared; those that tell lies, that jump into the domain of uncontrolled fantasy, will be burned. Thus, nearly all the books of chivalry, full of magical and supernatural events, are condemned—all except for a few, such as the *Tirant lo Blanch*, since in this one "knights eat and sleep, and die in their beds, and make their wills before dying, and a great deal more of which there is nothing in all the other books" (52). Even a pastoral novel such as the *Diana*, by Jorge de Montemayor, is not exempt from the rigor of exclusion: it will be saved for posterity, but only if the passages dealing with the wise woman Felicia and with the enchanted water are eliminated.

The determining factor in this literary trial is the conception of what is real and true. Ultimately, for Cervantes, everything that is perceived as reproducing a feudal epistemology needs to be not only discarded but actually stamped out of the social memory.[3] This is not to say that *Don Quixote* pretends to deny history. On the contrary, it is a book with a profound vision of historical development. Cervantes's novel aims at rewriting history, at forging a past with a sense of continuity that could, at the same time, justify a new attitude toward reality. Don Quixote's embodiment of medieval epistemology, "a living anachronism wandering through the plains of Castille," unveiled the inadequacy of the dominant ideology to meet the representation of reality. *El Caballero de la Triste Figura* must die, for "in last year's nest there are no birds this year" (828). The new social order required a precise differentiation between true historical figures, such as El Cid, of heroic but proportional di-

23

mensions, and fictional knights whose size and exploits failed to mesh with the "new perspective." Imagination had to correspond with reality, images with objects, art with the principles of common sense or reason:

> I have never yet seen any book of chivalry that puts together a connected plot complete in all its members, so that the middle agrees with the beginning, and the end with the beginning and middle. On the contrary, they construct them with such a multitude of members that it seems as though they meant to produce a chimera or monster rather than a well-proportioned figure. And besides all this they are harsh in their style, incredible in their achievements, licentious in their amours, uncouth in their courtly speeches, long-winded in their battles, silly in their arguments, absurd in their travels, and, in short, lacking in anything resembling intelligent art. For this reason they deserve to be banished from the Christian commonwealth as a worthless breed. (Cervantes, 374)

The creation of the bourgeois state in Europe was the culmination of a long process in which a new epistemology carved its space amidst the foundations of the old medieval world. This was a process that needed to discard, to banish from the ideological horizon, all vestiges of a feudal worldview. It was an act of exclusion which permeated all the structures of social life and which was embedded in the principles of the new bourgeois perspective. The Cartesian society, the reasonable and enlightened society, was to be built by silencing the unreasonable premises of the past, by relegating to darkness the irrational and superstitious universe of the Middle Ages. Otherness was reformulated and, at the same time, eliminated from daylight, bound to the past, condemned to the realm of chimera, *confined*.

For Michel Foucault, "the great confinement" of the classical age is one of the distinctive features of the enlightened society: "It is common knowledge that the seventeenth century created enormous houses of confinement; it is less commonly

known that more than one out of every hundred inhabitants of
the city of Paris found themselves confined there, within several months" (1965, 38). From 1656, when a royal decree in Paris
founded the Hôpital Général, thus creating the legal and physical structure of confinement, to 1794, when Pinel "liberated"
the madmen of Bicêtre, from the ascent of Cartesianism to the
fall of La Bastille, the new order rearranged its boundaries, re-
assigning the horizons of imagination. Unreason, the huge depository of medieval and feudal epistemology, was silenced,
cast out, and imprisoned in the outskirts, thus allowing the
city—which had become the new measure by which social life
was to organize its discourse—to become the model for the
bourgeois world. Just as imagination had to correspond with
reality, so too was the inverse required: reality had to conform
to the conception that bourgeois society had of itself. A series
of measures, therefore, was slowly implemented, not only to
transform socioeconomic relations, but also to restructure ma-
terially the physical social space. A new geography mapped out
the universe and the globe as well as neighborhoods and
streets. By the end of the eighteenth century, Jacques François
Guillauté tried to implement some urban reformations: Paris
would be divided in twenty *quartiers* of twenty sections each,
with twenty houses per section, each floor numbered individu-
ally, a letter assigned to each door. People were thus controlled
and confined to their concrete and respective coordinates
within the Parisian map.[4] At the same time, everything that
rested in the margins of order was excluded, erased from the
new dominant worldview as well as physically removed from
the urban center. Houses of confinement were located in the
periphery, for hospitals, workhouses, pauperhouses, and pris-
ons assumed the function not only of curing, educating, or
punishing, but also of hiding. Madness, indigence, and crime
were reduced to a single category and expelled from the visual
horizon. Even death, a familiar image in the Middle Ages, began to lose its role as a protagonist of everyday life. Philippe
Ariès notes that cemeteries began to abandon their familiar site

25

next to the city church: "There is no doubt that during the seventeenth century the umbilical cord that connected the church and the cemetery was loosened, without yet being cut" (1981, 321). By the eighteenth century, cemeteries such as Saint-Sulpice in Paris were being consecrated in the outskirts.

Confinement was not, of course, a sociopsychological abstraction suddenly taking shape in these houses of banishment and reclusion. Confinement, as even Foucault notes, was very much a part of the economic configuration of "classical" Europe; it belonged to mercantilism. "In the mercantilist economy, the Pauper, being neither producer nor consumer, had no place: idle, vagabond, unemployed, he belonged only to confinement, a measure by which he was exiled and as it were abstracted from society" (1965, 230). Criminals and madmen were thrown together with beggars and the unemployed; labor drew the frontier between illegality and acceptance, between deathlike seclusion and full existence. In his analysis of an anonymous eighteenth-century text, *Etat et description de la ville de Montpellier fait en 1768*, Robert Darnton notes the following: "Finally there were domestic servants and the unemployed poor. The author listed them after the laborers, but he excluded them from his classification scheme, because they did not have any corporate existence. . . . They lived outside of urban society and did not constitute an estate, although they could be seen everywhere swarming through the streets" (125). Between the people and the underworld (*le peuple et les bas-fonds*), eighteenth-century writers drew a line: work was, for the vast majority, the feature that separated those reasonable beings who participated in the productive effort from a fifth estate, composed of the "scum," *la populace*, always ready to rob or riot.

And yet this theoretical distinction was difficult to implement in practice, or even to sustain at the ideological level. Seasonal work, subemployment, home work, and so on were categories that introduced ethical nuances which, in the application of the "labor principle," were not always recognizable.

26

Other criteria were also needed and used in establishing the boundary. Henri Sauval describes the foundation of the Hôpital Général as follows: "It was given out that the General Hospital would be open on May 7, 1657, to all the poor who were willing to be admitted of their own free will and through the magistrates. By public cry the beggars were solemnly forbidden to ask for alms at Paris; never was an order so well executed. . . . on May 14 the poor were committed without the least trouble. The whole of Paris changed its appearance that day; most of the beggars retired to the provinces. . . . The most prudent of them decided to earn their living without begging and the frailest committed themselves of their own accord" (Chevalier, 118). If, on the one hand, productivity had been set as the demarcation between seclusion and existence, on the other hand Sauval uses poverty as the definitive line. The poor had to be excluded from the third estate, and the differentiation between working poor and idle poor will become, as we shall see, a very important issue in nineteenth-century politics. Already in the eighteenth century the problem had come to the surface. What the anonymous bourgeois of Montpellier was referring to had less to do with a work-related distinction than with a fundamental appreciation of poverty: "The common people are naturally bad, licentious, and inclined toward rioting and pillage" (Darnton, 130). Therefore, as Darnton notes, the society depicted is no longer divided into three estates but rather comprises two hostile groups inhabiting a world where "differences in language, dress, eating habits, and amusements" (131) *showed* the separation. True, the nonproductive members of the "lower" classes had been confined or expulsed, at least from the main cities; the marginal elements of society had been erased from daylight, or at least such was the attempt; and there was a general cleaning-up of the urban centers, emptied of their hospitals and cemeteries. And yet that other distinction of appearance would remain in bourgeois society, in a sense undermining its own effort at differentiation: laboring classes and "dangerous" classes would form an amor-

27

phous impoverished group whose shifting composition reinforced the unitary vision ultimately held by the dominant class. The borderline between the two categories was artificial and could not hide the fact that their members could easily cross it: "One can detect in many writers a presentiment of hate toward the *bas-fonds*, where the people, dehumanized by misery, lose their quality, where the *Opéra des Geuex* is nothing but a sign of the mutation of the laboring classes into dangerous classes" (Roche, 42). Thus, even though the politics of mercantilism had created a space for the nonproductive, in reality it sanctioned a stigma that would overflow and contaminate the bordering social groups. It is clear that in the development of cities, for instance, the trend was to eliminate the cohabitation by different classes of the same streets or buildings. The vertical distinction by floors was replaced by a horizontal displacement: laboring classes were pushed from the center to the periphery, to that same edge of the city in which stood the houses of confinement. On the eve of the French Revolution a notorious pauperization of the Parisian suburbs had taken place.

A culture of poverty, then, in the eyes of the bourgeoisie, united the different elements that formed the "popular classes": the "working trades" as well as the "poor and the miserable," to use the words of Daniel Defoe. This was a culture characterized by its primitiveness and savagery, by its inclination to crime, by disorder and chaos; a barbaric and foreign culture whose attributes coincided with or, more precisely, articulated a vision of insanity, since "madness, even if it is provoked or sustained by what is most artificial in society, appears, in its violent forms, as the savage expression of the most primitive human desires" (Foucault 1965, 193).

During the eighteenth century the city was never presented by the social imagination as a source of evil. This is not to say that there was not a recognition of the presence of specific problems, such as property crimes, health, and air pollution. Such problems, however, were always attributed to foreign causes. A siege mentality dominated bourgeois culture. Immigration, for instance, in spite of the fact that it was quantitatively small, acquired negative connotations as the vehicle of disorder. In Paris, Auvergnats or Gascons might at times be portrayed as exotic, sympathetic figures, but in general they were viewed as loud, violent, given to committing crimes. "The Parisians," writes Sauval in his *Histoire et recherches des antiquités de la Ville de Paris* (1724), "are friendly people, sweet-tempered and very civil. . . . Robberies and murders, insolence, blasphemies and similar disorders are far less common in Paris than is said and are usually perpetrated by soldiers or the dregs of the people, who are not Parisians" (Chevalier, 219). Crime, then, was marginal and alien, belonging to outsiders who brought it into a world conceived as the depository of reason; crime shared the same marginal space as the lower classes, those faubourgs at the outskirts where people "are more ill-disposed, quicker to take offense, more quarrelsome and more unruly than people in other districts," as the faubourg Saint-Marcel is described in 1781 (Chevalier, 219). Crime encircled the city, brewing at the edges, at that point of intersection between a rural world still reminiscent of medieval superstitions and feudal connotations, and an urban world symbolizing the new economic order.

The general trend during the eighteenth century, then, was to create a marginalized periphery in the social imagination that encompassed everything that rested outside of order and that by the force of association colored all the components with the same taint of unreason and threat. From madness to idleness, from crime to pauperism, from riots to the formation of the new working class, an identical global metaphor of the negation of order—the metaphor of unreason—would conceal them together. This trend, of course, implies a process, a gradual transformation of perception. There would be distinctions established during the eighteenth and nineteenth centuries, between the working poor and other poors. Patrick Colqohoun, for one, emphasized such a differentiation in England toward

29

the end of the eighteenth century, including in the criminal element only "the submerged class of the chronically poor or sick, the destitute, beggars, vagrants, *homeworkers*" (Rudé, 134; emphasis mine). And yet the association persisted and would, later on, become a serious issue within the working classes as they attempted to disassociate the proletariat from the lumpen. But in general terms the classical age is epitomized by the bourgeoisie's effort to rearticulate otherness. As we shall see, this articulation will be in constant need of reformulation of its own boundaries.

2

In 1763 the Parliament of France began preparations for the definitive transfer of cemeteries to the outskirts of Paris. The longstanding trend toward making the city an image of life, a universal sign of bourgeois achievements, acquired legal formulation. One year later, in London, the dead were returning to reclaim their space in the social imagination: in 1764, with the publication of Horace Walpole's *The Castle of Otranto*, the Gothic novel was born. Precisely at the moment when reason was reaching its apogee, when the process of exclusion seemed near completion, unreason reappeared on the scene. As Foucault notes, "classical reason once again admitted a proximity, a relation, a quasi-resemblance between itself and the images of unreason. As if, at the moment of its triumph, reason revived and permitted to drift on the margins of order a character whose mask it had fashioned in derision—a sort of double in which it both recognized and revoked itself" (1965, 201–2).

In the middle of the eighteenth century, cities in France and in most other European countries began to revive medieval fears about the plague. It was a panic that expressed itself in medical terms but that in fact responded to an ill-defined moral myth. The "great fear" had little to do with reality. Rather, it reflected a perception that illnesses as such were mysterious

plagues originating in the houses of confinement, at the outskirts of the city, and overflowing their boundaries to invade
the urban center. "The house of confinement," writes Foucault, "was no longer only the lazar house at the city's edge; it
was leprosy itself confronting the town. . . . The evil which
men had attempted to exclude by confinement reappeared, to
the horror of the public, in a fantastic guise" (1965, 202–3).

It was indeed a "fantastic" reappearance. In the first chapter
of Walpole's book, a wedding is taking place (a wedding that
assures the continuity of the protagonist's dynasty), when suddenly a giant helmet appears and kills the groom, thus casting
a shadow over the future of the house. The horror of the scene
comes not from the presence of death or of macabre descriptions, although they do contribute in creating the space of fear;
what the text singles out is the nature of the agent of death:
"The horror of the spectacle, the ignorance of all around how
this misfortune had happened, and, *above all*, the tremendous
phenomenon before him, took away the prince's speech. Yet
his silence lasted longer than even grief could occasion. He
fixed his eyes on what he wished in vain to believe a vision; and
seemed less attentive to his loss, than buried in meditation on
the stupendous object that had occasioned it" (28–29; emphasis mine)—an object which, as we later learn, is a ghost of the
past asserting his right to intervene in the present in order to
redress an act of injustice: his own murder and the expropria-
tion of his land. Within the microcosm depicted in the novel,
the tools of reason seem powerless, and order can be attained
only through the intrusion of the forces of unreason, by the use
of old and "supernatural machinery." This is astonishing, if one
remembers, as Tobin Siebers notes, that "in the eighteenth
century, the Rationalists worked to demystify all forms of supernatural representation, religious and magical, because they
associated it with the violence of social persecution" (123). Can
one be led to assume, then, that these works represent an anti-
bourgeois perspective? As we shall see, this is not the case since

31

one of the main features of Gothic literature is precisely its defense of order and its negation of arbitrary rule. The intrusion of unreason has a more ambiguous and problematic meaning.

In *Otranto*, as in Gothic literature in general, unreason materializes (or threatens to do so) within the walls of its own epistemological frames: castles, monasteries, old abbeys, dungeons. It is not in the lighted street, nor in the vastness of nature, neither in the city nor in the country, where reason is challenged: it is, rather, within the symbols of feudalism that the representation of unreason emerges. In Ann Radcliffe's *The Romance of the Forest* (1791), for instance, journeys of leisure into the Swiss Alps, or curative voyages across the Mediterranean, or even desperate trips to (and through) Paris are not cause for alarm. An old monastery, buried in the darkness of the forest, on the other hand, immediately creates the expectancy of the unreal or of undetermined fears: "Terrors, which she neither endeavoured to examine or combat, overcame her, and she told La Motte she had rather remain exposed to the unwholesome dews of night, than encounter the desolation of the ruins" (1:38).

No doubt monasteries' becoming places of fear expressed a logical correspondence in a society that had equated the Middle Ages with unreason, but such correspondence was not the only consideration for selecting such symbols. Tombs, for instance, also played an important role in the imagery of the Gothic—and not only because they brought death to the foreground, for death as such, as *Otranto* had already exemplified, was not horrific. It was the tomb itself, its physical as well as imaginary structure, that inspired uncanny feelings. Very often the representation of these sepulchres was anachronistic: thus, the grave Adeline finds in *The Romance*, with its subterranean construction, more closely resembles contemporary tombs than ancient ones. "The seventeenth and eighteenth centuries," claims Ariès, "presented another image of death: the subterranean vault, a large enclosed space that was not, like hell, another world; it was of the earth, but devoid of light, a *camara*

32

obscura" (1981, 347). The image of death, as that of unreason, rested in the corners of confinement.

The basic setting, then, the central spatial metaphor that sustains Gothic literature, is confinement: dark rooms, labyrinthine halls, and secret passages populate its pages and convey, as E. B. Murray affirms, the ambiguous idea that they serve "as a retreat from the real world and as a vestibule leading directly, through dream or fancy or secret panel, to the unreal" (94).[5] Castles and monasteries, tombs and secret rooms projected the images of La Bastille and Bicêtre, of hospitals and workhouses, to the extent that confinement came to represent a dominant ideological act, a cultural trait shared by the most "advanced" European countries. But the structure of confinement, as we have seen, formed part of a wider perception of social organization in which the world encompassed by unreason had been expelled to the margins of bourgeois order. The reappearance of these unreasonable forces, then, logically embodied not only the image of seclusion but also that of periphery.

The first reencounters with unreason during the last third of the eighteenth century translated into a central cultural metaphor, that of marginality. Gothic literature gave it a precise form; it fully articulated the notion of marginality, whether spatial or temporal. The settings of Gothic narrative are always either remote epochs (in *Otranto*, for instance) or distant, "peripheral," and "backward" countries (in Potocki's *The Saragossa Manuscript*, Radcliffe's *The Italian*). The symbols of the bourgeois world were not yet openly present within the framework of representation. The city and its streets, for instance, are conspicuously absent in this early production. In general, during the eighteenth century, "the evil came, or probably came, from one source which was not the city itself or its inhabitants. If the city was sometimes unhealthy . . . that was no fault of the urban environment itself, but was due to circumstances extraneous to the city or else to persons unknown and to the fact that the city adjoined backward and ignorant rural areas" (Chevalier, 148). Neither the city nor the country, but rather that no-man's-land in which the rural and the urban worlds met; neither the image of an agricultural society nor the locus of mercantilism, but rather that belt on which a new economic order was basing its resources and to which it was relegating its residues: this is the space from which the eighteenth-century Gothic was projecting its fears. The outskirts of the city, with their hospitals, their immigrants, their dangerous elements, their workers, and their poor, were at the same time the source of imagery and the recipient of it. A trip to the quartier Saint-Marcel in Paris, for instance, was seen by Sébastien Mercier as a voyage to the extremities of the known world, to a land peopled by animality and barbarism. Eighteenth-century writers plunged into the underworld to discover the existence of a primitive universe that needed to be civilized and tamed.[6] A dangerous universe inhabited by monstrous beings encircled civilization.

This idea of an alien yet proximate world, the image of periphery, is fundamental in understanding the fantastic representations assumed by the Gothic. Too much distance would not allow for a questioning of the premises of reason: "The fact that *Vathek* [by William Beckford] did not initiate any serious competition to the Gothic novel during the 1790's indicates that [the readers] came to demand more relevant human identification in their reading fare than they found in the thin and insubstantial fabric of Oriental fantasy. They wanted a supernatural somehow humanized by credible emotional involvements in situations where moral decisions were feasible" (Murray, 31). An Oriental extravaganza such as Beckford's created a distance that allowed either for dismissal or for allegorical interpretations, thus eliminating the bases for the recognition of paradox, of that "humanized supernatural" alluded to by Murray. The Gothic, on the contrary, appealed to a different problem. It recalled an otherness that lay next to the core of the bourgeois world, questioning by virtue of its tangential presence the nature of order. Gothic literature had to be based on the recognition of otherness—a process of distortion that later in the nineteenth century would become essential to the fantastic. Either through historical reconstruction or by reproducing the landscapes of more feudal countries like Spain or Italy, the intrusion of a medieval epistemology contrasted drastically with contemporary worldviews at the same time that it exhibited a familiar identification.

This intrusion, in a sense, also formed the basic structure of the ruins that populated the pages of Gothic literature. As a recurrent symbol, they not only allowed for representing confinement, but they did so by erecting a configuration in which nature and artifice were at odds: it was actually the space of neither but was rather an image of periphery. Ruins were neither the projection of an Arcadian countryside nor the emblem of civilization. They stood in a no-man's-land where the ivy romanced the stone, where two worlds intersected. And if neither the city nor nature could claim those ruins, both could recognize themselves in them. They were the perfect setting for monstrous apparitions, since they themselves were the articulation of monstrosity.

As perceived by the Age of Enlightenment, the monster was the image by which unreason penetrated order. The monster, says Marie-Isoline Marsaud in her analysis of Sade, was the barbarian, the foreigner, the one that introduced violence, madness, and disorder into a system considered to be the reign of pure reason (11). But the effectiveness of this disruption resided in the monster's conceptual proximity. After *Otranto*'s giant helmet, the incursions of otherness tended to be less eccentric. Clara Reeve's formula summarizes a pattern slowly adopted by successive Gothic writers, in particular by Ann Radcliffe: "There is required a sufficient degree of the marvellous to excite the attention; enough of the manners of real life to give an air of probability to the work; and enough of the pathetic to engage the heart in its behalf" (Murray, 33–34). Too much of any single element would project the work into already established categories, into allegorical or realistic representations. For the Gothic to be effective, dosage was ex-

35

tremely important since it afforded the possibility of creating the monster, that figure in which reason "both recognized and revoked itself." In the following passage from *The Romance of the Forest*, different elements appear associated: "Louis, though unused to fear, felt at that moment an uneasy sensation. . . . He advanced to the ruin, and called him. No answer was returned, and he repeated the call, but all was yet still as the grave. He then went up to the arch-way, and endeavoured to examine the place where he had disappeared; but the shadowy obscurity rendered the attempt fruitless. He observed, however, a little to the right, an entrance to the ruin, and advanced some steps down a dark kind of passage, when, recollecting that this place might be the haunt of banditti, his danger alarmed him, and he retreated with precipitation" (1:163). Louis, a professional soldier "unused to fear," experiences what can only be interpreted as apprehensions of the possible emergence of the supernatural, of unreason. The setting is a ruinous grave in which shadows obstruct the empirical recognition of reality. Faced with all these elements, a sudden association of ideas will make this brave soldier run away ("retreat with precipitation"): the possibility that the grave is haunted not by ghosts but by banditti. In effect, the substance underlying the projection of marginality referred to very concrete problems.

In a sense, the great fear that arose during the second half of the eighteenth century and that, according to Foucault, had its source in a moral myth about the plague was also the expression of a social concern, of a concrete political problem. Even if this fright adopted visions of the past, its birth was rooted very much in the present. It came, it was said, from the hospitals in the outskirts of the city. Coming from the periphery, it shared the same characteristics as the rest of the dreadful tensions emerging in the decades preceding the events of 1789. A challenge to order was emanating from the poor sectors of society. Sébastien Mercier, for instance, sensed the spirit of insubordination that was affecting the popular classes (Roche, 279). This "spirit" took the form of both criminal rebellion and political revolution; it would eventually find its contours in Paris, "un catorze juillet," but it had already haunted the major European cities.

It is not clear whether a rise in crime actually occurred at the end of the eighteenth century,[7] but what did increase was an awareness of its presence. If no quantitative change took place, at least there was a qualitative transformation. At the beginning of the eighteenth century, the image of the highwayman projected a justified sense of fear, but it was also dressed with a certain glamour, perfumed by an exotic attraction. Names like Dick Turpin joined other famous and more urban outlaws such as Jonathan Wild and Jack Sheppard to form a sympathetic myth cultivated above and beyond the popular classes.[8] During the second part of the century, however, the moral status of the outlaw declined, at least in the eyes of the dominant sector. Slowly he ceased to attract the Sunday visits of proper ladies to the cells of Newgate, in much the same way that lunatics disappeared from the dominical show.[9] When in 1773 *The Newgate Calendars*, the first extensive collection of criminal stories, was published, the objective of the book was clearly didactic: to show that honest work makes honest people. But the publication also revealed, through public exposure, the other side of the paradox: crime would no longer be considered an exceptional or isolated occurrence within the parameters of organized life; on the contrary, it would become a social classification, belonging to society, though attached to what had been constructed as the realm of otherness.[10] Crime began to lose its individuality in order to become an anonymous act committed in the city by elements of the "dangerous classes." From the highwayman to the crowd: this was the basic trend followed by the dominant culture in its perception of social danger. Thus, by the end of the eighteenth century, cities in Europe, at least in the most "advanced" countries, began to create or strengthen their police forces, assigning them the mission of repressing crime as well as of maintaining a general control over insubordination.[11] In 1782 in London the Foot Patrole, composed of sixty-eight men and attached to the Bow Street Office, was created in order to guard the streets at night. Ten years later, a small group of detectives, Mr. Fielding's People, was charged with the task of investigating and locating crime. Indeed it seemed as if confinement had become a useless act of contention: unreason was spreading into society.

Rioting became the clearest manifestation of this phenomenon. The French Revolution would incarnate, especially after 1792, the threat par excellence of unreason, since it "liberated" and opened up the streets of Paris, the cultural capital of civilization and Enlightenment, to the barbarous hordes. But the signs were already present. The Wilkes riots of 1763–1774, the 1766 riots in southwestern and midland England, the massive *guerre des farines* of 1775 in France, and the Gordon riots responded very often to traditional economic pressures and formed part of established patterns of popular protest. Yet they also expressed something new. These riots were not just a demonstration against a shortage of food but an attack against the social conditions that created it, against the Enclosure Act of 1760, which incorporated the rural sector into new economic relations, and against the introduction of machines in the means of production, a situation which would create unemployment.[12] "The crowds that halloo'ed for Wilkes, as a sign of elementary class hostility to the rich, celebrated their hero's return to Parliament by smashing the windows of lords and ladies of opulence . . . the Gordon riots . . . directed their attack against the properties of prosperous or well-to-do Catholics, while the poor Irish . . . were left strictly alone" (Rudé, 139–40). These revolts were manifestations of unreason not only because they were carried out by the popular classes, that amorphous and contradictory social category, but because they targeted the economic foundations of the new bourgeois order and came to resemble an incipient class struggle.

The specter of revolution, then, seems to be at the base of this reappearance of unreason in general, and of the fantastic in particular.[13] And yet it is a specter with many contradictory implications. In Radcliffe's *The Romance of the Forest*, for instance, Adeline attacks the foundations of tyranny and defends her right to rebel in a passage reminiscent of the American Declaration of Independence: "Since he can forget, said I, the affection of a parent, and condemn his child without remorse to wretchedness and despair—the bond of filial and parental duty no longer subsists between us—he has himself dissolved it, and I will yet struggle for liberty and life" (1:81). In *The Italian* Vivaldi opposes his father with very similar arguments, affirming those "few instances in which it is virtuous to disobey" (544). Despotic, medieval, unreasonable characters, such as La Motte, embodied, then, the image of the monster.[14] They represented evil figures whose arbitrary desires showed an absolute disrespect for the reasonable rules of society. Thus Adeline reflects on her situation: "O exquisite misery! 'tis now only I perceive all the horrors of confinement—'tis now only that I understand all the value of liberty!" (2:184–85).

The locus of unreason projects here all its ambiguity. Confinement, at the end of the classical age, symbolized unreasonable repression as well as the repression of unreason. Thus the storming of La Bastille on July 14, 1789, immediately became the emblem for posterity of bourgeois history. It marked the end of tyranny and the beginning of liberty. It was not the beheading of Louis XVI that tradition recorded as the gesture of liberation, but rather the demolition of a castle, of a prison which, as is well known, contained few prisoners. The demolition of confinement was an act that if, on the one hand, it liquidated the obsolete premises of the medieval world, on the other hand it served to unleash unreason. Bicêtre was "liberated," the "mobs" ravaged the urban landscape of Paris, installing the Reign of Terror and publicly demonstrating the ultimate consequences of the bourgeois revolution, Napoleon spread his popular armies through Europe. . . . The impulse of liberty was carried too far, opening the gates for the barbarians at the outskirts to take over. The history of the French Revolution became the history of Europe from the moment that it set the example not of bourgeois uprising but of popular power. As Gwyn A. Williams indicates, "no matter how radical the differences between the two countries, in both Britain and France, it was in 1792 that 'the people' entered politics" (4). From this moment, the restoration of reason would require a redefinition of its boundaries.

3

Capricho 43, as already mentioned, adhered to the principles of Enlightenment: those impossible monsters, as Goya calls them, could exist only outside of the domain of reason. A tension nevertheless resulted from the simultaneous representation of two incompatible systems in one single sign. This paradox, I have argued, was at the base of fantastic art. The ambiguity of the message of plate 43 seems to run deeper than this representational problem. The title itself ("El sueño de la razón produce monstruos") presents an enigma, since the word *sueño* in Spanish is ambiguous and can be translated as both "sleep" and "dream." An earlier sketch of *Capricho 43* contains a different inscription: at the base of the desk one can read "Universal Language. Drawn and Etched by Francisco Goya. Year 1792." At the top of the plate is one word: "Sueño." And the legend begins with the phrase "El artista soñando," a phrase which can only be translated as "The artist dreaming," since the present participle *soñando* does not carry the double meaning— *durmiendo* would have been the appropiate word for "sleeping." One can safely assume, then, that it is the dream and not the sleep of reason that produces monsters. Several critics, including Klingerder, López-Rey, and Paul Ilie, have already suggested this interpretation in their analyses of Goya's work. Even Baudelaire showed that he had perceived the same meaning when in his poem "Les phares" he referred to the *Caprichos* as "les cauchemars," the nightmares.

The semantic difference is a fundamental one. Instead of articulating a gesture of exclusion, *Capricho 43* suggests that there is indeed some continuity between the realms of reason and unreason, the latter being, in fact, a creation or product of the former. The distinction between dream and imagination had rested in the active presence of reason, which established truth and order. As defined by the *Encyclopédie*, "wake's imagination is a policed republic where the voice of the magistrate establishes order; dream's imagination is the same but in anarchy." Reason, that magistrate, separated both worlds: order from chaos, art from madness. How, then, could reason dream? It could rest, abandon its taming role, sleep; but it could never be on the side of anarchy. By creating those monsters, reason was negating its own essence, was questioning its most decisive attribute: the establishment of truth. This, as we shall later see, would eventually happen for Goya. The classical age could only approach this problem of reconciling opposites—without adopting mysticism—through perplexity or dazzle, since the acceptance of such an antinomy implied dismantling the foundations of Enlightenment, its "law of day and night," as Foucault calls it, "a law which excludes all dialectic and all reconciliation; which establishes, consequently, both the flawless unity of knowledge and the uncompromising division of tragic existence; it rules over a world without twilight, which knows no effusion, nor the attenuated cares of lyricism; everything must be either waking or dream, truth or darkness, the light of being or the nothingness of shadow. Such a law prescribes an inevitable order, a serene division which makes truth possible and confirms it forever" (1965, 109–10). The process of reconciliation, of joining vision and blindness, would fall into the category of madness and ultimately of nothingness, as Goya would illustrate in *Disaster 69*. But, as Foucault continually notes, this nothingness could manifest itself, could "explode in signs, in words, in gestures." This was a fundamental paradox, "for madness, if it is nothing, can manifest itself only by departing from itself, by assuming an appearance in the order of reason

41

and thus becoming the contrary of itself" (1965, 107). Was it then also possible that reason could manifest itself through the images of unreason?

In a sense, the *Caprichos* represent the opposite side of the same problem addressed by Foucault in his study of madness: if reason and unreason could form an indistinguishible unity, if each contained elements of the other, if the seeds of unreason were sown by reason, then the principles of exclusion and confinement had been not only false but useless. This was, indeed, a disquieting assertion, one that would eventually lead Goya to a life of isolation in his Quinta del Sordo and that would send into hiding Diderot's *Le neveu de Rameau*. If the simple presence of unreason within the boundaries of artistic discourse meant a negation of the exclusionary premises, then by establishing a relation of cause and effect between reason and unreason Goya did more than simply recognize the coexistence of opposites. He was in fact proposing that the horizons of order created the threat of disorder, that the bourgeois world actually produced its own menacing monsters. Goya's forms were not born out of nothing, out of madness, as Foucault claims. They were, rather, born out of reason, out of society. They were giving shape precisely to that vacuum, filling in the darkness of night with figures projected out of reality.[15] The priest's banishment of monsters from the imaginary in *Don Quixote* was done in the name of truthfulness to reality; under the same argument unreason was reentering fantasy almost two hundred years later. At this stage all these considerations appeared in Goya merely as a first approximation to the problem. After all, they were simply caprices, that is, sudden and unreasonable desires. Monsters were still said to be impossible, and it would be necessary to wait until *The Disasters of War* for Goya to further the exploration of the topic.

The dream of reason produces monsters; the "animal spirits" of and within order create chaos; the inner structures of society engender their own threat. Undoubtedly, the latter part of the eighteenth century experienced a sudden feeling of apprehension about the future. The absolute confidence with which the bourgeoisie had erected its monolithic universe suddenly began to crack. In *The Romance of the Forest* Adeline lives in a constant present inserted between an intimidating past and a menacing future, as if the entire novel were an interval in which to reconcile these two extremes: "Adeline, meanwhile, in the solitude of her prison, gave way to the despair which her condition inspired. She tried to arrange her thoughts and to argue herself into some degree of resignation; but reflection, by representing the past, and reason, by anticipating the future, brought before her mind the full picture of her misfortunes, and she sunk in despondency" (3:9). Adeline's life, needless to say, had not been a possible source of comfort. If she can reflect upon her past with a certain degree of astonishment (1:46), the real fear and terror lie in the shadows of a future enveloped by incertitude (2:139).

What were the causes of these representations of concern toward future times? Without any doubt the French Revolution, especially after 1792, spread the feeling of uncertainty about what would happen to the bourgeois world. At the ideological level, Malthus's *Essay on Population* (1798), for instance, denied the idea of progress, an Enlightenment presupposition that had led precisely to the formation of this bourgeois world. But the fears, whether expressed in medical terms, located in the barbarity of marginality, or projected toward the future, preceded these events and in a sense helped to create them. Their origin lay in a broader development in social thought and in a profound transformation of social and economic relations.

The same year that Walpole's *Otranto* appeared, Johann Joachim Winckelmann published his *History of Ancient Art*. This work was not a mere chronology of different periods or a descriptive report of diverse artistic creations. Instead, Winckelmann mapped out a system that would show how art originated, changed, and evolved from one form to another. Approximately at the same time, between 1749 and 1785, Georges-Louis Leclerc, Comte de Buffon, published his monumental *Histoire naturelle*. One of his important achievements was to extend the earth's age well beyond that suggested by the accepted biblical dates. With the 1779 volume, *Epochs of Nature*, Buffon departed significantly from the medieval idea of a single divine creation to outline a world of progress, change, and constant transformation. These efforts at establishing history fell, on the one hand, within the broader trend of consolidating bourgeois culture as the ultimate expression of civilization. But it also opened the way for the possibility of envisaging history as a process, a journey with different and contradictory stages, a procession whose characters are in constant transformation. The seeds that allowed bourgeois society to conceive of itself as another link in the chain of time were thus sown.

Adeline, in *The Romance of the Forest*, embodies this preoccupation: "Reflection, by representing the past, and reason, by anticipating the future, brought before her mind the full picture of her misfortunes" (2:139). This sentence could very well serve as the trademark of Gothic literature. It articulates a present sieged by the negation of the past and the threat of the future. Adeline, in the darkness and emptiness of her room, reads a manuscript she has found in a hidden chamber. The story (history) she uncovers parallels her own situation: an imprisoned man, who in the end will turn out to be her father, is waiting to be killed. This horrific reading, which reproduces the reading done by the actual reader of the novel, attains its full magnitude when it is understood as an example, a lesson in history that predicts future events. The manuscript's plot is thus interwoven with Adeline's adventures and is constantly interrupted by incidents from the present that serve to underline the connection between the two worlds.

Ruins play a fundamental role in representing the Gothic. Not only do they incarnate the image of marginality, of nature and artifice colliding, but they also project a perception of decay, of the ravages of time: "Several of the pillars which had once supported the roof, remained the proud effigies of sinking greatness, and seemed to nod at every murmur of the blast over the fragments of those that had fallen a little before them. La Motte sighed. The comparison between himself and the gradation of decay, which these columns exhibited, was but too obvious and affecting. 'A few years,' said he, 'and I shall become like the mortals on whose reliques I now gaze, and like them, too, I may be the subject of meditation to a succeeding generation' " (1:35). Of course, the topic of the effects of time was an old one. But within the context of the Gothic, the passage of time was no longer chronology, but progress. La Motte, a paternal and unreasonable medieval figure, is destroyed by capitalism and by his own ineptness at handling money. But the lesson to be inferred from the "sinking greatness" of feudalism was the projection toward the future: the possibility that the suprahistoric conception of the world of reason was also doomed to vanish. As Lukács affirms in *The Historical Novel*, "the often superb historical construction [of the Enlightenment], with its discovery of numerous new facts and connections, serves to demonstrate the necessity for transforming the 'unreasonable' society of feudal absolutism; and the lessons of history provide the principles with whose help a 'reasonable' society, a 'reasonable' state may be created" (20). It was, then, only a matter of applying the same principles, of pushing bourgeois thought to its logical conclusions. The reasonable society could, in turn, be transformed, and could eventually disappear. Reason as a monolithic, universal, and natural attribute of mankind began to be questioned when history introduced the possibility that the "self" could eventually become the "other." In the eighteenth century, nevertheless, the first fractures in the monolith were scarcely visible, and threats were still perceived as remote. For the time being, the dominant patterns for understanding reality remained suprahistoric. Reason, of course, corresponded to the epoch of civilization and progress, but within a vertical and idealist conception of history. One would have to wait, as Lukács demonstrates for the historical novel, until after 1815, until after the end of the Napoleonic wars, for the idea of historical progress to take hold in social thought.

45

That distance with which unreason reintroduced itself was confirmed through the metaphors of periphery. Unreason was the patrimony of primitiveness. Novels not only reproduced settings in the past or in "backward" countries but also presented conflicts as the result of transgressions or injustices that originated in an epoch outside the narrative frame. Thus, for instance, Manfred in *Otranto* is a villain not so much as a result of his own actions as by the fact that he is the heir of an usurper. Ultimately, reason always triumphed, whether formally, through the final rational explanation of seemingly supernatural events, or thematically, through the reasonable resolution of the narrative conflicts. But these narratives allowed unreason to emerge and, however briefly, cast uncertainty over bourgeois epistemology. As Foucault writes, "unreason reappeared as a classification, which is not much; but it nonetheless reappeared, and slowly recovered its place in the familiarity of the social landscape" (1965, 200). For a moment that might last only the length of a book, disorder threatened the principles of the reasonable society; for a moment, unreason was liberated from confinement and brought to the forefront of cultural representation.

It is no accident that this "liberation" occurred toward the end of the eighteenth century and not before. The emergence of Gothic literature in 1764 coincides, in general terms, with the beginning of the industrial revolution.[16] Foucault, as already mentioned, had already established a relationship between mercantilism and confinement: "The Pauper, being neither producer nor consumer, had no place [in society]" (1965, 230). With the coming of a new economic organization, manpower again played an important role. Gertrude Himmelfarb notes that "the decline of paternalism is generally associated with the rise of laissez-faire and the market economy, an ideology and an economy that broke the 'cake of custom,' the 'chain of connection,' the 'social fabric,' and set individuals free to pursue their own interests, in their own ways, for their own purposes" (189). This social liberation, preceding the political one symbolized by La Bastille and Bicêtre, removed poverty from the realm of nature and incorporated it into history: pauperism, as Himmelfarb continues, became "a product of the moral as well as the material advance of civilization" (148). In much the same way Foucault affirms that "madness was no longer of the order of nature or of the Fall, but of a new order, in which men began to have a presentiment of history" (1965, 220).

The same year as the American Revolution, Adam Smith published *An Inquiry into the Nature and Causes of the Wealth of Nations*. In it, Smith laid out the theoretical foundations that supported the industrial society; in it were explained the bases for understanding the material causes of progress; in it, too, were drawn the conditions of alienation of the working classes. The paradox exposed in that book resided in the proposal "that the division of labor, which provided the momentum for the progressive economy that was the only hope for the laboring classes, was also the probable cause of the mental, spiritual, even physical deterioration of those classes" (Himmelfarb, 55). Progress, therefore, functioned on the basis of contradiction, and the roots of conflict were engrained in its essence: the creation of a class whose worsening living conditions could result in an explosive social threat, as the numerous riots were in fact demonstrating. The dream of reason could definitely produce monsters.

"In a Romantic context, then, Gothic literature may be seen as expressive of an existential terror generated by a schism between a triumphantly secularized philosophy of evolving good and an abiding obsession with the Medieval conception of guilt-laden, sin-ridden man" (Thompson, 37). Without any doubt, critics in general perceive that the Gothic is the expression of some type of fracture—between order and chaos, between the natural and the supernatural. Heroes are portrayed as split between the sins of the past and the prospect of the future, people presented as victims both of themselves and of something outside themselves. Indeed, the Gothic articulates a chasm, one that was taking place in the "advanced" countries and that would tinge the entire nineteenth century. It was an economic as well as ideological fission (an episteme, to use Foucault's term) that opened up the world of modernity. The development of the industrial society would engender a series of contradictions that would intensify as the century advanced.

The Gothic occupies the first stage of the creation of the modern bourgeois society, that is, roughly the period between 1760 and 1815, between the industrial "takeoff" and the Congress of Vienna. It articulates the new tensions in society by reviving feudal imagery, a fact that creates an artistic paradox, for it is not the past that was feared but the visions at the outskirts of the future. And yet for that future to be conceived at all, a discovery of the past, of historical process, was necessary. The Gothic became a sort of archeology of fear, a sadistic (the term here acquires its full historical significance) unearthing and reconstruction of unreasonable forms. By giving unreason a kind of exposure, a displacement took place that allowed dominant society to control or tame the image of unreason, to tailor a moralistic dress around its presence. Yet this very act implied acknowledging its existence.[17] It is in this act and in this context, both as an expression of the problem and as a means of interfering in it, that the fantastic was born as an artistic discourse that would measure and define the cultural and political boundaries between reason and unreason.

III■ THREE ■III

1848:
The Assault on
Reason

1

FOR GOYA, the monsters of the *Caprichos* were still considered impossible within everyday life, within the parameters of reality. They existed only in the realm of visions, of dreams, of art. The legend in *Capricho 80*, the last one of the series, clearly states this: "If anyone could catch a denful of Hobgoblins and were to show it in a cage at 10 o'clock in the morning in the Puerta del Sol, he would need no other inheritance." But the plates themselves offer a somewhat different impression. The figures do not present clear contours; there are no orderly transitions between the different planes; the frontier between the images of reality and those of fantasy are blurred. For Baudelaire, these were the outstanding and significant features of Goya's art: "Goya's great merit consists in his having created a credible form of the monstrous. His monsters are born viable, harmonious. No one has ventured further than he in the direction of the possible absurd. All those distortions, those bestial faces, those diabolic grimaces of his are impregnated with humanity. . . . In a word, the line of suture, the point of junction between the real and the fantastic is impossible to grasp; it is a vague frontier which not even the subtlest analysis could trace, such is the extent to which the transcendent and the natural concur in his art" (430). As the French poet-critic implies, Goya's portrayal of unreason does not project into another time or space. It appears *hic et nunc*, here and now.[1] The chasm articulated by the Gothic seems now to be less relevant than the continuity, that line of suture in which dream and reality coincide. Goya reinforces the idea of proximity by bringing otherness almost within the frame of the self, and thus emerges at some points a certain difficulty in distinguishing the two systems, in differentiating the limits that the Cartesian world had meticulously traced.

The metaphor of marginality, so fundamental to the emergence of the Gothic, is therefore undermined by the way that unreason erupts onto the scene: unreason affirms its presence with feasibility, with confidence, as if announcing its right to coexistence and thus casting a shadow on the exclusive light of reason. Perhaps Goya, situated on Europe's "periphery" but embracing the principles of the Enlightenment,[2] had trouble establishing an imagery of differentiation. The fact is that the Napoleonic invasion of Spain in 1808 brought to the forefront the atrocities (the monstrosities) that a "civilized" country such as France was capable of committing. If *Los Caprichos* hinted, through an ambivalent representation, at linking reason and unreason, at reconciling day and night, then with *Los Disparates* and especially with *The Disasters of War* unreason acquired the status of reality. Goya, in this last production, did not discriminate: during the Peninsular wars, Frenchmen as well as Spaniards committed barbaric acts. In this sense the forces of civilization exhibited the same unreasonable values that primitive Spain had represented. Those impossible monsters of which reason dreamed suddenly materialized within the boundaries of the vraisemblable: "I saw it," says Goya in *Disaster 44*. This revelation created an epistemological crisis. *Disaster 79* affirms it categorically: "Truth has died." Number 80 raises a question that will hover over the following centuries: "Will she live again?"

After the Napoleonic invasion, Goya's production would be marked by an air of ambivalence. On the one hand, he achieved his great paintings about common people at work. *The Forge*, *Knife Grinder*, and *Girl Carrying Water*, generally dated 1817–1819, implied, according to Francis Klingender, that Goya "had defeated the monsters of reaction in his own mind even before

50

the collapse of political repression. For it is the spirit of freedom, the spirit of the dignity and joy of labour, as both Goya
and Shelley understood it, which emanates from these pic-
tures" (Licht, 66–67). Yet these monsters were not, as I have
said, the embodiment of reaction but rather the projection of
progress. Thus, on the other hand, during these same years
Goya withdrew to his Quinta del Sordo and delved secretively
into *The Black Paintings*, a strange series in which Saturn, the
god of time, cruelly devours everything he has created. The series would not be known to the world until many years after
the painter's death.

This dualistic outlook, on the one hand affirming the laboring classes, on the other envisioning an apocalyptic future,
would also dominate the bourgeoisie's worldview beginning in
the nineteenth century. Such a double vision was determined
by a political choice—either to accept that the principles of liberty and equality included the poor sectors of society, or to negate the idea of progress and find refuge in the same principles
of unreason that had been destroyed in La Bastille. For Georg
Lukács, these options became unavoidable after the events of
1848: "It was the 1848 Revolution which for the first time
placed before the surviving representatives of this epoch the
choice of either recognizing the perspective held out by the
new period in human development and of affirming it . . . or of
sinking into the position of apologists for declining capitalism"
(1962, 30). It was a choice, however, that was already present at
the turn of the century. In Goya it might have been only outlined, suggested, rather than openly proclaimed. Nonetheless,
within the pages of social imagination it was already a concrete
dilemma. Victor Frankenstein, for instance, must at one point
decide between acceding to the monster's reasonable requests
for justice and denying him his fundamental rights, between
procuring the creature's happiness and protecting the interests
of the human species.

This crisis, which would determine the distinctive marks of
fantastic literature during the nineteenth century, implied that

51

unreason was no longer just a simple category, acknowledged at the borders of order, but a real alternative present within the very premises of society. How did unreason move from a mere presence in the outskirts to a position from which it could question reason on its own terms and with the same rights? Why and how did unreason break through the boundaries that excluded it to invade and shake the very foundations of order?

2

In 1816, after the end of the Napoleonic wars, the Congress of Vienna reordered Europe. A new era was beginning. At exactly the same time, in Geneva, a now famous meeting took place. Byron, the Shelleys, and John Polidori agreed one night that each would write a tale of terror; a new epoch of fantastic literature was thus also born. Curiously, it was not the consecrated writers but the marginal characters in this literary séance who produced the two works that have since become cornerstones in the development of the fantastic: Polidori's *The Vampyre* and Mary Shelley's *Frankenstein, or The Modern Prometheus*. Polidori's work initiated a subgenre that would prove very popular and that would reach its fullest expression with Bram Stoker's *Dracula* in the final years of the century; Shelley's novel unbound a monster whose complexity and modernity still haunt our social imagination.

Some striking differences set these works apart from the Gothic, a genre that quickly faded away at the beginning of the nineteenth century. Unreason now seemed much closer and less peripheral; neither temporal nor spatial settings require feudal atmospheres or primitive surroundings. Frankenstein's monster does not need medieval chambers of confinement in order to emerge; he does not require monks and inquisitions in order to adopt a terrorific image. On the contrary, he moves about civilized centers and travels through Europe, retracing the Napoleonic invasions. In Polidori's novel, part of the action does occur in Greece, where in fact the vampire can openly demonstrate his supernatural powers, but contemporary London salons also make their appearance.[3] It seemed as though, little by little, fantastic literature undertook the inverse voyage represented in its eccentric pages: a concentric journey which would take unreason, through time and distance, from the periphery to the center, from barbarism to civilization.

Unreason appeared, therefore, *hic et nunc*. And yet during the first part of the nineteenth century, unreason was unable to fix its space of representation and alternated between the representation of old mansions of confinement and open streets, between primitive images of superstition and scientific laboratories of progress. This ambivalent depiction revealed an incertitude within dominant ideology in the identification of its own framework, and ultimately indicated a confusion in the recognition of the symbols of the self and of the other: "Alas! Victor," says one of the characters in *Frankenstein*, in a clear reminiscence of Goya's discovery, "when falsehood can look so much like truth, who can assure themselves of certain happiness?" (21).

In our present imagination, Frankenstein has come to designate the monster rather than his creator. This may be due in part to the fact that Shelley's novel deals basically with the formation of monstrosity, with the moral and political implications of such a category in the construction of the modern subject. The outcast, the banished or self-banished subject, the marginal figures that would constitute the central characters of romanticism, have contributed to the elevation of Frankenstein the doctor to the dimensions of his anonymous creature. But, rather than being merely an arbitrary historical rewriting, the confusion is rooted in an imprecise psychological differentiation between the two beings, which permits critics such as Harold Bloom to see the monster as Victor's alter ego. For Mary Poovey, such an indefiniteness reveals the familiarity of the monster, the subjectivity of otherness, thus allowing for the detection of a feminist discourse in Shelley's novel. In any case, the problem raised by the text refers to the proximity and continuity with which the self and the other relate. The monster is, one must not forget, the doctor's creation.

In 1828 in Paris, Vidocq published his memoirs. The book, which immediately became very popular, narrated his adventures as a police prefect under Napoleon. One of the first true detective stories, it summarized, in a sense, this difficulty in recognizing categories, since Vidocq himself, an example of the new hero in the fight against crime and the defense of order, had actually been, before his designation as commissaire, a notorious criminal in the same Paris he was charged to protect. Vidocq combined in his own persona principles of antinomy: police and crime, order and chaos, reason and unreason. The case of Pierre Rivière, a murderer studied by Foucault and his team of collaborators, is also exemplary. In 1835 Rivière axed his mother, his eighteen-year-old sister, and his seven-year-old brother to death in an attempt to save his father from the sufferings his mother and sister imposed on him; the little boy was killed because, in Rivière's words, "if I only killed the other two, my father though greatly horrified by it might yet regret me when he knew that I was dying for him, I knew that he loved that child who was very intelligent, I thought to myself he will hold me in such abhorrence that he will rejoice in my death" (1982, 106). The confusion that this monstrous crime provoked in bourgeois epistemology, as is evidenced by the court transcripts, lay not so much in the nature or essence of the crime as in the fact that Rivière *wrote* a confession explaining, with impeccable logic, his motives. Was he crazy and therefore innocent, or was he sane and therefore guilty? Could a monster expound reasons? If Rivière committed parricide as an act of liberation, should the Revolution's own regicide not serve as a precedent for acquittal? And if this was the case, how could monstrosity be any longer perceived as a category exclusively reserved for otherness?

It was not, of course, a legal problem. Rivière was convicted;[4] his death sentence was later commuted to life in prison, where he would commit suicide a few years later. This maneuvering allowed for both an exemplary condemnation of his acts and an absolution of his responsibilities. But the act of categorizing that had dominated the classical age, the enactment of a law of day and night, as Foucault described, was challenged. As these cases illustrate, the new gesture became a blurred attempt at differentiation: the frontiers between reason and unreason, the lines that designated the boundaries of confinement and exclusion, had lost their neat demarcation.

The elimination of the estate society and the changes brought about by the dual revolution (the Industrial Revolution and the French Revolution) indeed created a problem of recognition. Within the new economic configuration, it became more difficult to define social relations and to assign the proper images or the appropriate spaces to the different elements of society. As Gertrude Himmelfarb indicates, if the slogan for the latter part of the nineteenth century was "Educate! Educate! Educate!" then the motto for the beginning of the century should have been "Separate! Separate! Separate!" (398). The perception of social reality was tinged by confusion. A conflict in perception, in vision, prevaded the dominant culture.

The first necessary step in an attempt to clarify the situation was to try to differentiate clearly (as the bourgeois of Montpellier had done) the lower groups from the bourgeoisie, that new class which now defined the social norm. If this was particularly imperative in France, given the distorted impressions created by the "excesses" of the Revolution, other countries embraced an identical need. In England, for instance, in a speech to the House of Lords in 1831, Henry Brougham, the Lord Chancellor, provoked the anger of the Radicals when he spelled out the differences between the bourgeoisie and the lower classes: "But, if there is the mob, there is the people also, I speak now of the middle classes—of those hundreds of thousands of respectable persons—the *most numerous*, and by far the *most wealthy* order in the community . . . who are also the genuine depositories of *sober, rational, intelligent, and honest English feeling*" (Himmelfarb, 299; emphasis mine). Mob and people were the first and broader classifications from which to justify class distinctions in the new and equal social order. The "rational people" of the middle classes were characterized by a series of attributes that had to serve not only as the bases for their own definition but also as the pillars supporting a divisive line between them and the mob. Such a task was not easily accomplished, and the descriptive terms used by the Lord Chancellor were ultimately insufficient:

—Quantity served to justify political power now that quality had been decapitated—but it would logically also become one of the main arguments of the workers' movement.

—Sobriety was proposed as a sign of proper public behavior—but, as Doctor Jekyll would later illustrate, drinking was an "activity" difficult to assign to or contain within a particular class.

—Intelligence, that old barrier between man and animal, could serve to rationalize the dehumanizing conditions under which the lower classes survived—although it would be through the discourse of reason that the bourgeois order would be challenged.

—Patriotism could mask a norm, "nationalize" the values of those middle classes—and yet "the paradox of nationalism was that in forming its own nation it automatically created the counter-nationalism of those whom it now forced into the choice between assimilation and inferiority" (Hobsbawm 1975, 104).

Of all the posts erected by the Lord Chancellor to delimit the two worlds, only two remained as useful indicators: wealth and honesty. The two terms maintained an intricate association as the century advanced. For the dominant culture at large, wealth symbolized order. It traced an unblurred vertical distinction, the ultimate line of social separation, although it was also a dangerous sign to bring to the forefront of the ideological battle. Honesty, on the other hand, especially for the liberal bourgeoisie, assumed a more convenient role, since it also established a horizontal differentiation—or at least attempted to do so.

At the beginning of the nineteenth century, numerous legal undertakings, and continual cultural and political debates, dominated the "poor question." If it was difficult to establish clear patterns of differentiation between dominant and marginal cultural values, when it came to applying the separate motto to the lower classes, the ambivalence and confusion persisted, if it did not increase. The end of mercantilism implied the end of confinement. "With the nascent industry which needs manpower," writes Foucault, the pauper "once again plays a part in the body of the nation" (1965, 230). In England, the New Poor Laws were passed in 1837. In 1838, the London Working Men's Association drafted the People's Charter: Chartism, according to Himmelfarb, "proposed to bring the poor into history by making them active participants in history, the authors of their own history" (269). But who were these poor? Did they consist of everyone on the other side of the wealth line, or could some nuances be established within the realm of poverty?

Without any doubt, the ideological effort was directed toward compartmentalizing this vast sector of the population. There were, for instance, the "respectable laboring classes," as Mary Carpenter, the founder of a "ragged" school, called them before the Select Committee on Juveniles in 1852, emphasizing "the very strong line of demarcation which exists between the labouring and the 'ragged' class, a line of demarcation not drawn by actual poverty" (Himmelfarb, 378). The intent was clearly to avoid a single quantitative distinction based on wealth by emphasizing an ethical difference that would add a qualitative variation within the ranks of the poor. Thus, diverse terms like "poor," "pauper," and "ragged" were used in an effort to distinguish those that complied with social norms—that is to say, those who worked and followed social directives such as the ones espoused by Henry Brougham—from the drunks, the beggars, and the criminals.

It was a futile effort. As Himmelfarb once again notes, "the intention [of the New Poor Laws] had been to remove the stigma of pauperism from the poor by confining it to the pauper class. The reality turned out to be quite the reverse. A stigma so visible and obtrusive could not be so neatly contained. In spite of all the efforts to distinguish, separate, and segregate pauper and poor, the stigma attached to the one inevitably tainted the other" (175–76). The royal commission created in London in 1834 to examine the social problem presented by poverty accepted that, in current usage, "poor" was assigned to the self-sustaining laboring class and "pauper" or "indigent" to the recipients of charity. But such a theoretical assumption could not be enforced except under experimental conditions; both categories could not be visually distinguished in everyday life. Workhouses and reformatory schools then became a kind of laboratory for applying and confirming the principles embraced by the dominant ideology: poors and paupers were physically separated, material conditions were controlled so as to create two distinct life-styles, and so on. The entire effort was directed at incorporating the workers within the parameters of the reasonable society by assigning to them all the values—except wealth—promoted by the bourgeoisie, and casting out of society the rest of the members of the disqualified classes. This was to be achieved without appealing to confinement. Hence the promotion of reformatory entities that could "recycle" into society a manpower endowed with the belief that indigence was not only punishable but shameful and disgraceful. Idleness not only remained stigmatized but, much as Pinel had done with madness, was "liberated" from confinement and internalized by the individual, extracted from patronage and thrown into the streets of a "free" society.

The end result of this confusing dualistic approach (one aspect of which worked toward differentiating, while the other opened the possibility of crossing the lines of demarcation) was to unite under the same banner the entire segment of society that lay on the other side of wealth. Radical and worker movements would therefore try to emphasize their own lines of demarcation within the ranks of poverty. The first demand of the People's Charter read: "A vote for every man, twenty-one years of age, of sound mind, and not undergoing punishment for crime." Women, the insane, criminals, and minors were not included in what constituted, at least from a political perspective, the "people." For the dominant cultural apparatus, however, as Disraeli denounced in 1837, poverty was a crime. And poverty, ultimately, was a general category that included beggars as well as workers and delinquents.[5]

Thus, in spite of all the "liberations," in spite of all the efforts undertaken at the beginning of the nineteenth century to separate the deserving laborer from the "scum," one thing remained unchanged: in the social imagination, unreason was still inhabited by the shadows of poverty, by the worker as well as the beggar, by the destitute, the mad, the drunk, the criminal. These characters still represented barbarism, primitivism, otherness. Accordingly, the same metaphors that during the last part of the Enlightenment had articulated, in a fantastic guise, the threat of unreason remained present in the new age of industrialization and modernity. During his visits to the low quarters, Mayhew saw himself as a traveler through the unexplored country of the poor, and established comparisons between the latter and the nomadic tribes of the Songuas and the Fingoes.

And yet some fundamental differences began to appear. Thus, for instance, when the same Mayhew wanted to identify the nomadic "species" native to London, he listed the streetsellers, street-buyers, street-finders, street-performers, streetartisans, and street-laborers. The old image of marginal and confined barbarism was transformed into a public display of savagery. Such a cultural change was marked and conditioned by the events in France at the close of the eighteenth century: "In certain respects the Revolution looks like a settlement of scores between two groups of the population, the old Paris bourgeoisie and the rest—those who used to be called savages, barbarians or vagrants, of whom it was stated in a petition put forward by some bourgeois in 1789 concerning the Montmartre charity workshops: 'They were truly a horde of savages within reach of the most civilized city in existence.' *With the Revolution, the savages entered and remained in the city*" (Chevalier, 222–23; emphasis mine). Revolution, then, came to signify the ultimate image of unreason, the incarnation of all the elements that shaped unreason. Revolution meant monstrosity. And after 1816, the perception was that "revolutions constitute necessary, organic components of evolution" (Lukács 1962, 28). Hence monstrosity was intrinsically attached to the principles of order; it belonged to the "self."

3

In 1848, at Fox Farm in the state of New York, the first séances of modern spiritualism were conducted. That same year, across the Atlantic, Marx and Engels published the *Communist Manifesto*, with the now famous introductory sentence, "A spectre is haunting Europe—the spectre of Communism." The language of esotericism connects two apparently unrelated events. When Marx adopted an image of the fantastic to depict a concrete political phenomenon, he was both using dominant discourse as well as deconstructing a cultural metaphor; he was referring to a new attitude in bourgeois culture as well as pointing out the ultimate source of this posture. In this sense, then, the introductory sentence of the *Communist Manifesto* reveals the extent to which the imagery of the fantastic was shaped by and gave form to concrete problems. Marx and Engels endowed unreason, as far as it implied a negation of bourgeois order, with a definite political name; they assigned to those specters which populated the imagination a concrete space and time. The phantom was hic et nunc, in contemporary times and within the geographic boundaries of the "advanced" European societies. Suddenly, the marginality with which otherness had engaged its first incursions dissipated in the words of a program that openly proclaimed the true identity of the monster. Prince Prospero, in Edgar Allan Poe's *The Red Death* (1842), protects himself from the plague that surrounds his palace by erecting walls lined with armed guards and camouflaging his guests with smiles of diversion. Prince Prospero might have perpetuated the Gothic belief in peripheral threats and acted accordingly; and yet at the end, not only would he discern amidst his guests the unpleasant presence of a death mask, but he would also discover that behind the disguise of that red death stood, in effect, the red death.

However, even if the *Manifesto* depicted without any disguise the terms of the conflict, even if Prospero proved that adopting the mask of unreason was a sign of unreason, bourgeois culture continued to attempt to postpone the unveiling of naked truth, relegating to the other side of a reinforced ideological barrier all the elements that haunted its existence. Throughout the nineteenth century, Europe portrayed itself as plagued by vague fears that tinged the imagination with colorful but imprecise menaces. Toward the end of the century, Arnold Boeklin's *The Four Horsemen of the Apocalypsis* would condense and summarize a vision of fear forged decade after decade. These fears covered the entire color spectrum. The German writer A. Wirth remarked, "Formerly it was the French who made our blood boil; in recent times it is now the Americans, now the Red International, now the 'Gold International' that makes us tremble; now the Russian bear that tries to eat us up, now the English boa-constrictor that means to strangle us. The 'black' or 'brown' danger has been in fashion since the Herero War. . . . At present the huge 'Yellow Dragon' is worked up and threatens to darken our skies like a powerful comet. But even that is not the end" (Gollwitzer, 172). What all these fears ultimately shared was the suggestion that the social order was in danger, even though daily experience did not indicate the presence of a threat. The empirical "testing" of social reality was not sufficient to dissipate the beliefs ingrained in bourgeois culture. It was not important whether there existed, in the Rhineland as in England, a concrete and direct possibility of the destruction of order, because at this stage in the development of the industrial society, dan-

ger revealed an attitude toward order itself more than a reaction to immediate threats: "Just as the European middle classes
of the 1840's thought they recognized the shape of their future
social problems in the rain and smoke of Lancashire, so they
thought they recognized another shape of the future behind
the barricades of Paris, that great anticipator and exporter of
revolutions" (Hobsbawm 1975, 11). Attached to the system as
an ontological part of it, destruction could manifest itself in
unreliable or unbelievable forms, but it would always be there,
casting a shadow over the future and the prosperity announced
by the comfortable universe of the bourgeoisie.

In opposition to the perception of the classical age, the seeds
of destruction—which the Gothic had always portrayed as
coming from the margins of order—were accepted by the new
industrial epoch as sown within its premises. *The Fall of the
House of Usher* (1839), by Edgar Allan Poe, has been frequently
read as a representation of the decline of reason.[6] But Usher's
house is a place as well as the embodiment of a dynasty, Roderick and Madeline being the last two representatives: "[the] appellation of the 'House of Usher'—an appellation which
seemed to include, in the minds of the peasantry who used it,
both the family and the family mansion" (63). From the very
beginning, then, the text establishes an identification between
the house and its owners; thus, the crack along the walls that
the narrator notices upon his arrival parallels the fissure in
Roderick's mind and anticipates the double final collapse of
mansion and protagonists. As the narrator soon discovers, the
causes of Usher's troubles form an intrinsic part of his being:
"[Roderick Usher] entered, at some length, into what he conceived to be the nature of his malady. It was, he said, a consti-
tutional and a family evil" (66). The house is, then, the palace
of reason inhabited by unreason as well as the individual's rational mind demolished by madness.

This genetic determination offers the possibility of explor-
ing at least two roads of interpretation. On the one hand, the
descent into madness unearths a journey into primitiveness,

discovering insanity at the root of "man's" psyche. In this sense, it implies a voyage back in time to a precivilized state. On the other hand, by identifying person with house Poe endows the mansion with a symbolic value: it is reason overpowered by unreason. Hence it also suggests the collapse of the reasonable premises of bourgeois epistemology. In this sense it alludes to the role of unreason in shaping society's future, thus uncovering a social and political issue. As with the Gothic production, the recall of primitiveness, of "backwardness," announced the form of things to come. The problem now resided precisely in locating and determining those forms, in assigning an appropriate imagery.

Unreason during the eighteenth century moved around the urban periphery, overtaking the nonproductive sectors, touching the rural immigration, caressing in general the poor population—a population whose members were considered to be foreigners and regarded, as Chevalier affirms, "as not belonging to the city, as suspect of all the crimes, all the evils, all the epidemics and all the violence" (365) in a kind of tautological argument that made of crime an external threat, and of every alien a potential criminal. The street people of the nineteenth century were different: if they still represented barbarism, they now belonged to the city. Eugène Sue opened his *Mystères de Paris* (1842–1843) by calling the reader's attention to the fact that the barbarians and the savages he would be introducing did not belong to remote countries but were to be found "among ourselves." Reynolds's *The Mysteries of London* (1845–1848) would follow a similar pattern with a savage depiction of the English "low" life. In fact, just as the Gothic's tendency was to reproduce medieval and "backward" settings, the new scenery in popular literature became, especially after 1848, the "unknown country" of the bas-fonds.[7]

This internalization of monstrosity by the dominant culture would still maintain, during the major part of the nineteenth century, a certain ambivalence, as if the social imagination hesitated and was incapable of deciding what image to assign to unreason: either to completely mask otherness or to blur the lines of separation between the self and the other. For Thomas Plint, in his *Crime in England* (1851), there was no doubt that the metaphors of danger referred to an inner origin spreading like a cancer through society: "The criminal class live amongst, and are dove-tailed in, so to speak, with the operative classes. . . . They constitute a pestiferous canker in the heart of every locality where they congregate" (Himmelfarb, 387). For Saint-Marc Girardin, on the other hand, the image of suburb was still present. As he wrote in the *Journal des débats* of December 8, 1831, "Every manufacturer lives in his factory like the colonial planters in the midst of their slaves, one against a hundred, and the subversion of Lyons is a sort of insurrection of San Domingo. . . . The barbarians who menace society are neither in the Caucasus nor in the steppes of Tartary; they are in the suburbs of our industrial cities" (Hobsbawm 1962, 238). Whatever the preferred image, heart or suburb, two common elements emerged as depicting the new social representation of threat: first, emphasis was placed upon the proximity and internal character of unreason; second, a definite association was established between danger and the working classes.

Saint-Marc Girardin was deconstructing—in much the same way that Marx and Engels would later deconstruct contemporary specters—the metaphor of marginality, stressing the discovery of unreason within the frames of order, as if the masking undertaken by the Gothic had been not only inappropriate but also deceitful.[8] Girardin's portrayal of social conflict, however, still maintained some of the old characteristics, alluding to the suburbs as the origin of the threat. Without any doubt, this was an image that remained in the cultural projections of the bourgeoisie, especially during the decades preceding the 1848 revolutions. Balzac, for instance, at the end of *Ferragus*, referred to this suburban world as a source of tensions, "for here it is no longer Paris; and here it is still Paris." And yet these outskirts were no longer perceived as a moat between two worlds but rather as unreason's Trojan horse. The spreading plague feared by the Gothic had definitely anchored some tentacles within the realm of order.

This happened, in part, because of the identification of danger with the lower classes and, more precisely, with the laboring classes. Thus, for instance, as Hobsbawm notes, "the men who rose against the bourgeoisie in the Paris of 1848 were still the inhabitants of the old artisan Faubourg Saint-Antoine, and not yet (as in the Commune of 1871) those of proletarian Belleville" (1962, 253). In spite of their not being proletarian, as Hobsbawm himself notes, the men and women who raised the Parisian barricades were identified by the bourgeoisie with the generic name of "working classes" (1962, 146). The economic pressures of the new industrial age were "proletarianizing" the poor, thus making more difficult the possibility of establishing differentiations, at least from the perspective of the dominant ideology. An identification, then, between Saint-Antoine and Belleville was possible: "An even greater difficulty in drawing a distinction between the laboring and the dangerous classes is that some of these intermediate groups, or those regarded as such, did not work and live in distant workshops or building sites in the banlieue, but in the center of the city, cluttering the streets and squares with their trade, their rags and their noise. They thus forced everyone in Paris personally and concretely to be daily aware of the existence of a nomadic way of life in the very heart of the city" (Chevalier, 369). As the different elements of the poor classes became associated, the spatial configuration of unreason modified itself; what had been reserved for the suburbs was now also applied to other more centric neighborhoods, thus giving way to the cancer image without having to abandon the siege metaphor. Furthermore, the latter would be a metaphor that would find a concrete realization in the urban reforms of the second half of the nineteenth century. The construction of wide boulevards was motivated, in Paris as in London and other major European cities, by the need to destroy these concentrations of undesirable elements within the daily bourgeois habitat.[9] La Place de Grève, for instance, a symbol of crime for the Parisian imagination, changed its name to Place de l'Hôtel de Ville and, little by little, lost its old connotations, until they completely disappeared with the reforms undertaken by Haussmann. The old District de la Cîté was completely destroyed and its inhabitants evicted to the suburbs, as if the bourgeoisie were continuing to try to reconstruct the locus of unreason, to contain it at the margins of civilization.

As Prince Prospero proclaimed, this was a futile effort. Unreason, that broad category that included every aspect of threat to the productive activity of society, came to adopt an image sustained almost exclusively by the presence in society of a revolutionary danger. Thus, Eugène Roch would exclaim: "Ah, Paris! You are cured of the cholera, but you are close to civil war; you are still sick indeed." As Louis Chevalier explains, "the rising in June 1832, coming as it did immediately on the heels of the epidemic, was in every respect merely the political continuation of a single biological crisis so far as the principal actors, the main places and the fear propagated throughout the city were concerned" (16). Indeed, as the century advanced, something was definitely changing in the bourgeois portrayal of unreason. This change was brought about by drastic modifications in social organization as a result of the dual revolution. In spite of all the debates, the dominant ideology was identifying "dangerous" with laboring classes. At the same time, these working classes were developing a political consciousness as workers. Therefore, by the 1830s and especially after 1848 there was no doubt that popular revolts were organized movements aiming directly at the destruction of order. As Rudé shows, protests progressively lost their "old" mercantilist connotations to acquire characteristics that linked them to the new industrial society (147–48).

The threat to order, then, came suddenly coupled with the idea of industrial development. Horror did not require the appeal of a medieval world since it now found images of unreason that also alluded to a more immediate context. When unreason was portrayed as a plague or a cancer spreading over the cities of progress, the metaphor was also referring to concrete problems, such as pollution. Thus, for instance, Eugène de Monglave, describing in his *Livre des lois* different Parisian issues, wrote: "The gibbet was abolished many years ago. Its site is covered by a cesspool where the excrements of Paris are deposited and where the horse butchers work. What was a place of horror in the old days is a place of disgust today; once they hanged men there; now they slaughter horses" (Chevalier, 212). The "reappearance of the suppressed" that characterized the dynamics of the Gothic lost its feudal connotations, and what now returned to haunt the amiable Parisians was their own residues: "Paris was described as a sick city . . . and much of the denunciation was directed against the sewers, drains and hospitals, all the places where the refuse of daily living piled up. . . . Correlations which . . . were not always imaginary, were established both in fact and in public belief between the places involved and social dangers [such] as sickness, poverty, crime and prostitution; and riots and revolutions too" (Chevalier, 206). Unreason, then, comprised the entire spectrum of threats, from sickness to revolutions. But clearly, unreason was now the product of society. Urban life was, without any doubt, a standard of civilization, at least when applied to certain quarters; but urban life also meant enduring the pestilence of concentration, or the possibility of catching "la maladie anglaise"—a form of melancholia that drove people to suicide and whose name derived from the fact that it was perceived as having been a result of economic development. Industry produced the material goods that allowed for a more comfortable existence; but it also generated the smoke that clouded bourgeois reality. Industrial development brought with it a future of wealth and progress; but it also engendered a working class that would challenge the foundations of such development. Political, social, economic, and medical categories were fused into a single image of unreason when they questioned or challenged the established order. The representation of an under-

world waiting in ambush, of a fissure underneath the respectable city, contaminated the dominant worldview during the major part of the nineteenth century.

In the summer of 1851 William A. Drew, a respectable Bos-
tonian, visited the London Great Exhibition. It was his first
trip to Europe, and he wrote a detailed account of his journey.[10] Parts of his description resemble a true fantastic story.
Following a path similar to that of Poe's narrator in *The Fall of
the House of Usher*, Drew descends through labyrinthine streets
to the darkest center, not of a mansion, but of London:

> As I have said, it was near night-fall when we set out for Field
> Lane Ragged School. We proceeded in an easterly direction
> some distance, towards a valley that lies between Holborn Hill
> and an eminence on the other side, on which are Smithfield,
> Newgate Prison and the Old Bailey. This valley is the lowest part
> of the city; and the great sewer under it conducts all the waste
> water and filth of London that are brought into it by lateral
> underdrains, into the Thames. This is the valley of Hinnom—
> the Gehenna of London, as I shall show, by and by. On our
> way thither, as we approached this miserable locality, signs of
> poverty, vice and crime became rife, and we began to feel un-
> pleasantly. It was the close of the Sabbath, working people were
> at leisure, the weather was clear and warm, and the inmates of
> the filthy dens that lined the streets were poured out upon the
> sidewalks and pavements, embracing reckless men, abandoned
> women, and dirty, naked children of all sizes and both sexes.
> (168)

This "miserable locality" was the same sector that the famous
outlaw Jack Sheppard used to control:

> All the buildings in this valley came, in some way, under his
> [Sheppard's] control, and were occupied by an army of thieves
> and robbers subject to his orders. The sidewalks had trap doors
> set in them; and whenever a man, supposed to have money,
> passed, suddenly the trap sprung and he fell into a cellar where
> he was instantly seized and strangled to death. . . . So many were

68

robbed and murdered in this way . . . that finally a righteous mob assembled in great numbers and tore every house down: and there "the Ruins" are now, with perhaps a hundred arches beneath them just high enough for a person to crawl into on all fours. These now are the only homes of hundred[s] of wretches of both sexes and of all ages. They sleep in these filthy holes by night, and saunter forth from them by day to steal and commit other villanies. (170)

All the appropriate elements of a fantastic atmosphere (ruins, trapdoors, secret cellars) are present in the description in order to announce the appearance not of supernatural monsters but of wretches just as monstrous and unreasonable, descendents of famous criminals such as Sheppard. Poverty, vice, and crime were immediately amalgamated into a single category and associated with working people "at leisure" to produce an indeterminate feeling of uneasiness. Even the time of day contributed to accomplishing this objective; it was near nightfall, which is an adequate setting for the new expression of the fantastic, as shown, for instance, by the beginning of *The Fall of the House of Usher*.[11] A sense of blurriness, of confusion, then, permeates Drew's account: London, the great metropolis of the world, the site for the Great Exhibition of bourgeois progress, offered at the same time a contrasting spectacle of degradation and danger. But these were not perils coming from the outskirts, from the houses of confinement at the edge of the city. The new image of danger arose from underneath the urban world, from the "lowest part of the city" and the "lowest" groups of society. Threat was no longer besieging the city; it had entered and now resided in the city's bedrock. It was as if unbound unreason had abandoned marginality to draw a definite fissure in the foundations of order. And as Drew's "fall" into the underworld progressed, the emanations from the sewers gave way to a recognition: the rats that inhabited this universe at night metamorphosed during the day into the robbers and villains of the London streets.

The dream of reason definitely produced monsters. This par-

69

adox, which at the end of the eighteenth century represented only a blurring of bourgeois vision, now announced the real possibility of an eclipse. The new industrial age created its own negation. Marx and Engels developed an entire political program from this premise, elaborating on the material conditions as well as on the imagery of contradiction: "The development of Modern Industry, therefore, cuts from under its feet the very foundation on which the bourgeoisie produces and appropriates products. What the bourgeoisie, therefore, produces, above all, is its own grave-diggers" (46).

Frankenstein's creature is thus not only a psychological projection but also, as Franco Moretti has shown, the embodiment of industrial production: he was built, literally, as a result of scientific and material advances. Movies have given us a monster tailored to a proletarian image which does not correspond with the novel's depiction. Such a transformation—which is in itself revealing about the perception of monstrosity during the first decades of the twentieth century—was possible in part because Shelley's book already alluded to this question. Frankenstein's monster traveled through the European countryside not only retracing the Napoleonic invasions but also incarnating the incursions of industrialism into the "harmonic" universe of peasants and fishermen, inspiring fear and chaos by his mere presence. The response that the monster's intrusion elicits from the people is reminiscent of certain attitudes toward industrialization, in particular that of the Luddite movement, which reached its apogee during the first decade of the nineteenth century. The "obscure and Satanic" mills of the industrial revolution, as Richard Astle points out, silently gravitate in Shelley's novel (71).

For S. L. Varnado, "Mary Shelley suggests, in fact, that some of the evil nature of the monster is the result of economic and moral dislocations in society" (65). If reason produced monsters, then it is easily understandable that a sense of culpability would arise among those of the dominant culture. Mayhew insisted upon this: "If the London costers belong especially to the 'dangerous classes', the danger of such a body is assuredly an evil of our own creation. . . . I am anxious to make others feel, as I do myself, that *we* are the culpable parties in these matters" (Himmelfarb, 327; emphasis mine). Such an affirmation had already been formulated prior to Mayhew's work and actually formed part of the generalized belief. On April 12, 1836, the *New York Herald* addressed the famous Robinson-Jewett murder with the following editorial: " 'The question now before the public involves more than the guilt of one person': it involves the guilt of a system of society—the wickedness of a state of morals—the atrocity of permitting establishments of such infamy [brothels] to be erected in every public and fashionable place in our city" (Schiller, 59). Victor Frankenstein discovered an identical truth. If Shelley's novel, on the one hand, leaves no doubt as to the criminality of the monster, since he kills innocent people, his monstrosity, on the other hand, could no longer be neatly attributed to external causes and had to be shared by Frankenstein himself: "How they would, each and all, abhor me and hunt me from the world did they know my unhallowed acts and the crimes which had their source in me!" (176).

This definite internalization of otherness, this final inclusion of unreason within the parameters of reason, implied not only that monstrosity was "real," but that it actually formed part of reason. The monsters were possible because "we" were the monsters. Victor and his creature, the representation of science and progress, and the projection of crime and destruction were all part of a single unit standing in a precarious equilibrium. The final elimination of the monster would inevitably mean the death of the doctor. They represented a single system in which evil and good intermingled, in which the separation of characteristics was difficult to grasp: "I [Victor] wandered like an evil spirit, for I had committed deeds of mischief beyond description horrible, and more, much more (I persuaded myself) was yet behind. Yet my heart overflowed with kindness and the love of virtue. I had begun life with benevolent intentions. . . .

71

Now all was blasted" (86). "When I [the monster] run over the frightful catalogue of my sins, I cannot believe that I am the same creature whose thoughts were once filled with sublime and transcendent visions of the beauty and the majesty of goodness. But it is even so; the fallen angel becomes a malignant devil" (209–10). Satan is a fallen angel; human beings are at the same time virtuous and vicious, magnificent and abject. Such a portrayal of unreason, after its banishment from history, necessarily created a sense of confusion and ambiguity. The old polarization between good and evil that had been effective in the Gothic tales disappeared with the progressive internalization of the demonic. As a result of this process, an epistemological uncertainty arose in bourgeois thought, a crisis that was articulated through and tamed by the fantastic, and that, as Rosemary Jackson shows, very often appeared in artistic representation in the form of madness, hallucinations, or multiple divisions of the subject. This uncertainty gave expression to the dichotomy that, as mentioned at the beginning of this chapter, confronted the representatives of the epoch. They, as Victor, were forced to choose between the happiness of their creations and the protection of their own species—that is, between accepting the consequences of their philosophical principles and defending their class interests.

This choice affected the entire bourgeois political spectrum. Even liberalism did not have clear theoretical defenses with which to face this contingency. For Hobsbawm, all the 1848 revolutions "were, in fact or immediate anticipation, social revolutions of the labouring poor. They therefore frightened the moderate liberals whom they pushed into power and prominence—and even some of the more radical politicians—at least as much as the supporters of the old regimes" (1975, 10). Thus, the implantation of peace and order through "unreasonable" repressive measures would be preferred to the ultimate development of democratic theories when these meant an assault on the socioeconomic organization of the bourgeoisie.

If confinement had been the gesture characterizing preindustrial society, it was now uncertainty which defined the attitude toward unreason. Undoubtedly, the space of unreason had become more difficult to delimit, spreading as it had from confinement to the sewers, undermining the foundations of order. But what definitely blurred bourgeois perception was the fact that unreason had acquired a discourse—a fact that in itself was contradictory, since discourse implied, by definition, the discourse of reason. "The most effective and powerful critique of bourgeois society," claims Hobsbawm, "was to come not from those who rejected it (and with it the traditions of classic seventeenth-century science and rationalism) in toto and *a priori*, but from those who pushed the traditions of its classical thought to their anti-bourgeois conclusions" (1962, 310). Marx and Engels spelled it out in writing and claimed the support of science. In 1848, with the *Communist Manifesto*, an "unreasonable" political program coincided with a revolutionary movement to foredoom, through an expropriated voice of reason, the end of reason: "The weapons with which the bourgeoisie felled feudalism to the ground are now turned against the bourgeoisie itself. But not only has the bourgeoisie forged the weapons that bring death to itself; it has also called into existence the men who are to wield those weapons—the modern working class—the proletarians" (41). The battles in the streets were now framed by another struggle: a philosophical challenge had arisen from within the framework of the dominant discourse. In the course of a few decades, what had been secluded broke its silence and managed to create its own voice from within. Reason, then, found itself in the locus previously assigned to unreason. "Je est un autre," Rimbaud would affirm later in the century, expressing an identity crisis that would progressively exacerbate the difficulty in distinguishing the double from its referent.

The adoption by many fantastic stories of apocalyptic endings might, at one level, have represented a metaphorical reunion of this divided self; but it also alluded to a resolution of the dilemma affecting the dominant classes: self-negation, destruction of their own postulates. And yet if this attitude was a vision of the solution, it also unveiled the bourgeoisie's inability, at this stage, to solve the problem at the theoretical level. As Carol Becker notes in regard to Poe's narrations: "Wakefulness/sleep, rational/irrational, conscious/unconscious—these are the primary forces in these narratives. They vie for dominance. But the battle between these polarizations is the only order that still remains" (66).

Once again, the idea of historical process assumed a key role in reshaping bourgeois consciousness. If the perception of historical change had been merely a spark that touched off the Gothic genre, by the middle of the nineteenth century it was becoming a hypothesis on which a vision of the future could be based—a negative vision that those same apocalyptic endings helped sustain. It was, of course, during this period that Marx's dialectical materialism and Darwin's theory of evolution erupted onto the European scene. The first acknowledged the idea that capitalism created its own contradictions; the second that "man himself" was nothing but the product of a biological process. Civilization, then, could be considered just another step on a never-ending chain of transformation;[12] human beings, nothing but the end result, the direct continuation of animality. With time, the self could actually become the other. How, then, could the bourgeoisie envision its own future? What lay ahead for "humanity"?

Mid-nineteenth-century thought, nevertheless, did not yet project a definite nihilistic attitude. There existed a deep concern about the future, about the ultimate results of progress, but the scale had not tilted in favor of total pessimism: "The battle between polarizations was the only order that still remained." The assault on reason, epitomized by the 1848 events, had been checked. A status quo resulted that would wait in need of resolution. For Himmelfarb, during the early periods of industrialization, "it was change that impressed itself more upon the consciousness of most contemporaries. And that sense of change was unnerving and disturbing, all the more so

because there was no end in sight" (137). Change would become an increasingly prominent obsession in bourgeois
thought, and the images of transformation and metamorphosis
would cover the cultural horizon. In *Frankenstein* Mary Shelley
clearly exposed this idea of mutability:

> We rest; a dream has power to poison sleep.
> We rise; one wand'ring thought pollutes the day.
> We feel, conceive, or reason; laugh or weep,
> Embrace fond woe, or cast our cares away;
> It is the same: for, be it joy or sorrow,
> he path of its departure still is free.
> Man's yesterday may ne'er be like his morrow;
> Nought may endure but mutability!
>
> (93–94)

Where, then, was essence to be located? Baudelaire would
find no alternative but the refuge in allegory:

> Le vieux Paris n'est plus (la forme d'une ville
> Change plus vite, hélas! que le cœur d'un mortel) . . .
>
> (78)

> Paris change! mais rien dans ma mélancolie
> N'a bougé! palais neufs, échafaudages, blocs,
> Vieux faubourgs, tout pour moi devient allégorie.
>
> (80)

4

The process of internalization that I have been underlining
shaped the characteristics of the fantastic during the first two
thirds of the nineteenth century. At the beginning of the twentieth century, it would culminate in a cultural production in
which unreason would be indistinguishable from reason, and
in which reality would be presented as nonapprehensible. In
the meantime, the two systems coexisted and overlapped,
drawing diffused contours at the line of suture, questioning

each other's validity, but remaining ultimately distinguishable. Unreason had infiltrated the space of order and offered itself as an alternative.

The paradox of representation that dominated the early fantastic acquired now the full status of an epistemological antinomy. Reality, as defined by preindustrial relations of production, saw its arrogant affirmation of supremacy undermined by the shadows implicit in its own assertion of progress. The fantastic articulated this paradox and offered to the public the disquieting possibility that reality was a problematic entity with several, and even contradictory, layers of signification.

Jean Baptiste Baronian defines the fantastic of this period as *le fantastique réaliste* because supernatural manifestations were presented within the coordinates of reality and as having an internal origin. In Mérimée, rational explanations were just as valid as irrational ones; in Balzac, the supernatural was always rooted and always appeared in a realistic framework. Even Eugène Sue shared these premises; his novelty, his art, according to Baronian, resided in the fact that he managed "to create an equilibrium between the fantastic myth and reality—a concrete, tangible and ordinary reality" (88). In other words, Baronian alludes to an artistic expression that presented as equally acceptable two sets of opposing worldviews. This dichotomy produced an inquiry into the self, at both the social and individual levels, that revealed the complexity and difficulty of knowing the "I." Once the vestiges of the old economic system promoted by the ancien régime had been demolished, once the traditional depository of otherness had been eliminated, any contradiction, any questioning of the new terms of reality had to lead necessarily to a self-questioning. How to reconcile the image of the Restoration with the egalitarian vision of the Enlightenment? The pages of the fantastic, with their diffuse contours, shadows, and uncertainties, would be traversed precisely by a problem of vision, of recognition.

Poe was probably the most significant representative of this period of the fantastic. His production, characterized by a struggle between polarized forces, alternated between different universes, reproducing the signs of confinement and the open streets, mythical settings and contemporary backgrounds.[13] In Poe, reason did not appear as the supreme ruler of truth, and the return to order was not, as in the Gothic, guaranteed. The American writer used accepted cognitive models to parody the reliance on the rational mind as the creator ex nihilo, in Becker's words, of the universe:[14] unreliable or mad narrators, thematic incongruences,[15] and similar uncertainties populate Poe's stories, undermining, as Pierre Rivière had undermined, what was considered the clearest representation of the discourse of reason—writing itself. In *The Black Cat* this self-undermining of authoritative discourse is clearly expounded: "For the most wild, yet most homely narrative which I am about to pen, I neither expect nor solicit belief. Mad indeed would I be to expect it, in a case where my very senses reject their own evidence. Yet, mad I am not—and very surely do I not dream. . . . Hereafter, perhaps, some intellect may be found which will reduce my phantasm to the common place— some intellect more calm, more logical, and far less excitable than my own" (140). As the narration unfolds, however, the temperate and reasonable depiction of unreasonable events inverts these postulates, and the reader is cornered into acknowledging the possibility of their occurrence. The end result of these subterfuges is a difficulty in recognizing and separating two systems that appear not (as in the Gothic) tangential to each other but overlapping.

The monster in the Gothic tale always maintained a recognizable profile. True, at times there were shadows that, instead of displaying monstrosity, suggested it; but ultimately, all the fleeing figures found a concreteness, a definition that rooted them either in this world or in the other. Not so during this period of the fantastic, where monstrosity exchanged places and bodies without clearly affixing its image: Who was the true monster, Victor or his creature? In *Usher*, Madeline, the strange and vague white figure at the very heart of the man-

77

sion, is Roderick's twin sister, thus projecting once again, as in *Frankenstein,* the idea of the double.[16] Given this confusion, this doubling of identities, how was monstrosity portrayed? What were its features?

The monster assumed two tendencies. On the one hand, it emerged in the literary imagination as an imprecise figure. Very little is known about Frankenstein's creature, except that he is too big, too ugly, and dressed in clothes (the doctor's) too small for him. On the other hand, it was presented as a normal human being. Polidori's vampire, for instance, did not deviate in looks, language, or dress from the standard gentleman. Carmilla, and many of Le Fanu's monsters, were indistinguishable from other members of society except for slight deviations, such as paleness or sharp teeth. Yet their behavior and morals revealed their monstrosity. In general, the monster was offered as a simple perversion of the human image, as a physical or psychological distortion of the bourgeois norm. In this sense the image of the monster did not differ much from the conception that dominant culture imposed upon the lower classes. As Arthur Harding would ironically comment apropos of his life in the East End underworld, "the whole thing was having your poverty well known to the people who had the giving of charity. . . . If you wasn't poor you had to look poor. The clothes you wore had to be something that didn't fit. . . . But you had to be clean" (Samuel, 24). After all, normality and even humanity were defined by male bourgeois standards. Thus, street folk were considered "parodies of bourgeois man" (Himmelfarb, 391), and the poor in general "were talked of as though they were not properly human at all" (Hobsbawm 1962, 236).

When William Drew visited a ragged school he was impressed by its inhabitants: "Most of the pupils were children from six to fifteen years of age; but some, I noticed, were gray headed men and women—objects almost too frightful to approach as if they were human beings" (171).[17] The alienation and reification of the worker were problems openly addressed during the nineteenth century. By losing his humanity, the proletarian entered the universe of unreason; from there, he became a threat. The paradox arose from the nature of social and economic organization. "I am malicious because I am miserable," said Frankenstein's monster. And those *misérables* were the direct product of society. Proudhon continually repeated this idea in his speeches: "When the worker has been stupefied by the fragmentary division of labor, by serving machines, by obscurantist education; when he has been discouraged by low wages, demoralized by unemployment and starved by monopoly. . . then he begs, he filches, he cheats, he robs, he murders" (Chevalier, 269).

The two positions within the dominant class were then reconciled. Either by nature or by nurture, for conservatives as well as progressives, either to condemn or to justify, the "lower" classes formed a monstrous category (comprising beggars, murderers, and workers) intrinsically attached to the bourgeois society and indispensable to its subsistence. This category, created by reason in its own image, and in the negation of its own image, inhabited the world as the concave reflection of bourgeois order. Such were the paradoxes that the revolutions of 1848 unmasked.

But this concave reflection—the poor-as-caricature, as Harding implied—also showed the ultimate resemblance of the poor and the rich. Dominant culture thus singled out traits that could define and, at the same time, justify social difference. During the second part of the nineteenth century, Cesare Lombroso, in his studies of criminological psychology, recognized the criminal type by certain characteristics that very often alluded to racial distinctions. Lombroso may have limited his "scientific" findings to the criminal; yet, as Hayes indicates (116), those characteristics were also applied, in daily use and in reports and articles, to the worker. These were features that would also appear in the portrayal of fantastic monsters: frequent gesticulations and ape-like agility (Frankenstein's monster, in spite of having been created several decades before, was

described in these same terms; and an ape was the murderer of
the Rue Morgue!), sharply pointed ears and sharp teeth (vampires), hairy bodies (wolf-men), and so on.

Distortion was thus a new mechanism in the fantastic by
which the frontiers between the real and the unreal became definitively blurred. And yet, by its essence, distortion served not
only to portray monstrosity but also to reveal the familiarity of
those images of unreason. Just as the contours of norm were
recognized in "the other," so too could the signs of monstrosity be discovered in "the self." Therefore, it is not strange that
fantastic representations adopted some introspective tendencies. As Rosemary Jackson affirms, fantastic literature "progressively turned inwards to concern itself with psychological
problems, used to dramatize uncertainty and conflicts of the
individual subject in relation to a difficult social situation" (97).
In this light, the intrusion into Usher's internal world acquires
all the characteristics of an exploration of the subconscious: the
narrator enters the house and descends through its labyrinthine
hallways until the image of tension is finally located—it is the
ghostly figure of Madeline.[18] Of course, a systematic and scientific study of the psyche would not be formulated until the latter part of the century, but the grounds for the discovery of the
sources of unreason within the self were already laid out.

Once the internal, endemic nature of monstrosity had been
acknowledged, not even the house (the home) could serve as a
secure shelter. Prince Prospero had not been able to keep death
from striking while the constant sound of the ticking of a clock
served as the reminder of an inevitable future. The assault on
reason ran through the entire spectrum of bourgeois life,
reaching its far corners as it questioned the self and the images
of affirmation that served to displace the ancien régime. From
banishment and confinement to ambiguity and uncertainty;
from marginality to distortion; from acknowledgment to alternative: unreason was internalized and, in the process, a transformation in dominant epistemology began to unfold.

80

|||| FOUR ||||

1917:
The Eclipse
of Reason

1

In November of 1895 Konrad von Röntgen discovered some rays with properties that had never been imagined. They were called X rays, a nameless designation for these mysterious beams that contradicted entrenched scientific concepts. Within a few days the discovery made headline news all over the world. Four months later, Becquerel discovered radioactivity. The society of iron and coal, of locomotives and steamboats, the tangible society, was rapidly transforming into a more ethereal world: the Generation of Materialism, as Hayes calls it, of the last third of the nineteenth century would better be represented by electricity, "something bordering on mystery" (93).

In 1905 Einstein published his special theory of relativity (the general theory was to come in 1916), shattering the Newtonian concept of the world. Between 1914 and 1918 World War I presented the world with a horrifying spectacle of technological and mass killing. In October 1917 the Soviet Revolution triumphed, bringing into power what was to become a stable communist government. A decade later, in 1929, the world economy collapsed. In the span of approximately thirty years, the scientific, moral, political, and economic universe of the bourgeoisie seemed to have fallen into chaos. The forces of unreason appeared to have taken over the universe of order.

During the same period of time, the avant-garde—the complete amalgam of "isms"—erased the premises of the realistic contract. The role of the nonrational, both as a philosophical

81

question and as the praxis of political alternatives, became the focus of a central debate in Western thought.[1] The fantastic—or marvelous, if one follows Todorov's distinctions—extended its area of influence to become one of the dominant trends in the new art. For Georg Lukács, Kafka's work represents the prototype of modernism since it centers on portraying "this experience, this vision of a world dominated by *angst* and of man at the mercy of incomprehensible terrors" (1973, 297). Once merely a presence at the margins of order, the signs of unreason now formed the central representation of bourgeois culture. Indeed, a profound "metamorphosis" appeared to have taken place.

Of course 1917, the year of the Soviet takeover, must assume in this trail of revolutionary landmarks the symbolic representation of this new period of the fantastic. But the turning point in the evolution may be identified with the events of La Commune in Paris in 1871, since here for the first time, even if only for a brief period, a workers' government, an "unreasonable" government, was in power at the center of the bourgeois world: "The Paris Commune . . . was important not so much for what it achieved as for what it forecast; it was more formidable as a symbol than as a fact . . . it was a brief, and in the opinion of most serious observers doomed, insurrectionary government of the workers in a single city, whose major achievement was that it actually was a *government*. . . . If it did not threaten the bourgeois order seriously, it frightened the wits out of it by its mere existence" (Hobsbawm 1975, 183). This government was short-lived and was closely followed by a period of turmoil. La Commune set the example. Under its shadow, Europe lived under a growing cloud of anxiety that permeated all aspects of social life,[2] an anxiety that was also sustained, after 1874, by an economic depression that darkened the entire panorama. Riots, strikes, and other forms of social and political action were numerous, presenting an organizational front (comprising parties, programs, associations, and so on) that finally made the idea of a successful workers' revolution feasible. After the Parisian events, as Rudé shows, "many more thousands of workers—and not only the cadres—had been won for socialism" (129). From *sans-culottes* to *ouvriers* to *prolétaires*, a specter was definitely inserting itself and spreading amidst the factories of order. By the end of the century, the dimensions of the threat posed by the lower classes were evident, and Gustave Le Bon, for instance, clearly addressed the issue: "The entry of the popular classes into political life—that is to say, in reality, their progressive transformation into governing classes—is one of the most striking characteristics of our epoch of transition" (15). "Society" seemed to be on the fringes of disappearing, thrown back "to that primitive communism which was the normal condition of all human groups before the dawn of civilisation" (Le Bon, 16). The ideological foundation of the bourgeoisie began to show the depth of its cracks. In the final decades of the century, the threat of revolution was indeed a specter completely implanted within the framework of dominant culture.

La Commune, in spite of the impact it had on the social imagination, did not produce a particular body of literary fiction directly related to it. And yet its influence, as Paul Lidsky demonstrates, would gravitate over the entire artistic production of the last quarter of the nineteenth century. The same cultural metaphors forged out of the streets of Paris in 1789 and 1848 would continue their presence and trajectory. In *Tableaux du siège, Paris 1870–71*, Théophile Gautier described La Commune using the language that the fantastic had carved in the realm of representation:

> Under every great city there are lion cages, caverns sealed with thick iron bars that contain wild animals, stinking beasts, poisonous beasts, all the refractory perversities that civilization hasn't been able to tame: those that like blood, those that enjoy stealing, those for whom attacking decency represents love, all the monsters of the heart, all the deformed souls; it is a filthy population, unknown during daylight, that move sinisterly in

the depths of the underground darkness. One day, a distracted keeper leaves the keys in the cages' doors, and the beasts invade the frightened city. From the open cages emerge the hyenas of 93 and the gorillas of La Commune. (Lidsky, 47)

From the obscure depths that had been undermining the cultural capital of civilization, from the sewers of Paris, those monsters that could not be seen at "10 o'clock in the morning in the Puerta del Sol" invaded the City of Lights. Beasts that fed on blood at night, primitive beings with "distorted" souls that offended the principles of morality—all the monsters unleashed in 1793 had resurfaced in 1871. They did so encompassing all the features of unreason, assuming the forms of either sickness or insanity—"an access of furious envy and social epilepsy," says Maxime du Camp (Lidsky, 46)—of primitive bestiality, of superstitious threat. But now, without any doubts or hesitations, unreason was reincarnated in the faces of the popular class: "History tells us, that from the moment when the moral forces on which a civilisation rested have lost their strength, its final dissolution is brought about by those unconscious and brutal crowds known, justifiably enough, as barbarians" (Le Bon, 18–19). Barbarism had finally reached the heart of "civilization" and had assumed, after many futile attempts at masking it or excluding it to the other side of the walls, its true name. For Paul de Saint-Victor, in *Red Orgy*, "a gang of obscure beings, known for the first time by the sign they carried on their shoulders, beings reminiscent of those masked or disguised bandits (such is the extent of their obscurity) that escalate at night the houses they are going to loot, take over Paris . . . invade the unarmed city. . . . La Commune established itself over the cadaver of that inert city" (Lidsky, 61). The symbolic act of La Commune consisted of offering a concrete example of the imaginary projections that had been evolving since the dual revolution: everything that had been confined to unreason replaced order. For a period of time, the threat of unreason was not a dream, nor an assault, but became the replacement of reason.

And yet the perceived monstrosity of the invasion of civilization evoked an equally barbarous response. The drastic measures taken to put down the Parisian revolution proved to be just as irrational as the events they were silencing. The massacre of revolutionaries and workers implied a total transformation of the reasonable premises that had inspired the reasonable society. Thus, precisely at the time when unreason seemed abruptly unmasked, at the time when the specters of industrial development were bluntly acknowledged without any epistemological bashfulness, the boundaries of reason disappeared.

2

Fantastic art incorporated the new factors shaping bourgeois perception. Robert Louis Stevenson's *The Strange Case of Dr. Jekyll and Mr. Hyde* (1886) is a case in point. On the one hand, it reproduces many of the features of fantastic literature written during the "assault on reason," and a series of parallels can be established with, for instance, *Frankenstein*: the space of representation is decisively contemporary, and unreason no longer inhabits only the places of confinement but also walks the open streets of the city, the framework of the modern landscape. Like Victor's creature, Mr. Hyde is the result of a search for transcendental knowledge, the product of scientific experiment and technological development—in short, the product of progress. And like Frankenstein's creature, the contour of his monstrosity is imprecise, indefinite: "Mr. Hyde was pale and dwarfish, he gave an impression of deformity without any nameable malformation, he had a displeasing smile . . . and he spoke with a husky, whispering and somewhat broken voice; all these were points against him, but not all of these together could explain the hitherto unknown disgust, loathing, and fear with which Mr. Utterson regarded him" (365). Mr. Hyde's profile does not present clear abnormalities. On the contrary, his monstrosity is determined by a distortion of the bourgeois image and character, a distortion that at times borders on caricature, and he is described simply as wearing clothes that, although made of rich and sober fabric, are enormously too large for him in every measurement.

On the other hand, new connotations emerge in Stevenson's novel, revealing it to be a different manifestation of the fantastic. Hyde, for instance, does not incorporate a single distinctive trait, such as the ugliness of Victor's creature, that could justify the repulsion he immediately provokes. It seems as if, in this selective evolution of the monster, its unmasking would only serve to demonstrate its elusiveness; its discovery would only serve to prove the difficulty in assigning it a space of demarcation. Increasingly, invisible monsters such as the monster of *Le Horla* (1887) would "materialize" within the pages of the fantastic.

This impossibility of assigning a locus to otherness, this impossibility of naming (encountered also by Röntgen) an unreasonable and mysterious reality, asserted itself as a fundamental premise of bourgeois thought. It was actually a characteristic that spread through dominant culture, allowing the fantastic to abandon its generic constraints and invade artistic production in general. Humans were immersed in angst; and if on the one hand they could recognize the causes in the immediacy of revolution, on the other they seemed incapable of representing the framework and face of the threat. Lovecraft's stories, for instance, would be characterized precisely by that impossibility of naming a "thing" which, as Rosemary Jackson points out, can only be registered textually as an absence. Maupassant had to make a real effort to invent a name that could only vaguely define the new being in his life: "Cursed is man! He is here . . . the . . . the . . . what is his name? . . . the . . . it seems as if he were shouting his name in my ear and I cannot hear it . . . the . . . yes . . . he is shouting it . . . I am listening . . . I can't hear . . . again, tell me again . . . the . . . Horla I heard . . . the Horla . . . it is he . . . the Horla . . . he is here!" (1925, 85). But what was the Horla? Where did it come from? What did it look like? Fear, without any doubt, was present, and yet its recognition faded away. As Maupassant says in *La peur*: "A vague fear slowly took hold of me: fear of what? I had not the least idea. It was one of those evenings when the wind of passing spirits blows on your face, and your soul shudders and knows not why, and your heart beats in bewildered terror of some invisible thing, that terror whose passing I regret" (1925, 238).

Within the metaphors of the fantastic, unreason had been using different masks to introduce itself in society. It progressively undressed, as the century advanced, until the moment when it could finally disclose its face. As Goya had already predicted in *Disaster 69*, the unveiling of the portrait of unreason showed its ultimate form: *la Nada*, nothingness. "Satan," says Marcel Brion, "is pure emptiness, the essence of vacuum, void and the vertigo of void. Vacuum has no forms but it is capable of assuming them all" (113). Thus, the images of the fantastic were capable of embodying the most common objects or situations of daily reality. For Maupassant, the furniture, decorations, and even kitchen utensils of a country house could inspire incomprehensible fears. A glass of water sufficed to put in motion the entire universe of the fantastic: the Horla, that thing/being without name or tradition, expressed itself through objects that behaved improperly, outside the logic of a pretended universal order. Fantastic occurrences ceased to be exceptional episodes and became plausible events of everyday life.

The fantastic modified the stage on which it had previously manifested its questioning of the principles of reason. The places of confinement had been slowly fading away; from the spatial and temporal margins of the Gothic, unreason now extended its presence through the entire social landscape. Thus, for instance, both in *Le Horla* and in Henry James's *The Turn of the Screw* (1898) unreason emerged in places that would not be considered conducive to its appearance. The two country houses where the action takes place do not present any menacing signs. On the contrary, they offer indications of assurance: they are at a secure distance from the city where the seeds of tension germinate. In fact, in *Le Horla* an opposite effect is adopted when the trips to the city eliminate the symptoms of anxiety. Where, then, should the source of unreason be located?

The country houses that Maupassant and James depicted did not project, of course, any sense of a medieval or feudal world. They are images of leisure, of unproductive retirement, places of rest where the bourgeois can escape from the unbearable social conditions that he himself created in the urban centers. The country house is, for all intents and purposes, an extension of the city residence, and the appearance of disorder within its walls shows the extent to which it was impossible to escape from the meanacing tentacles of unreason.

Unreason was definitely internalized; it constituted an onto-logical part of the bourgeois universe. As Dr. Van Helsing says about the vampire in *Dracula* (1897), "it is not the least of its terrors that this evil thing is rooted deep in all good" (146). The incarnation of a menacing otherness arose from within the foundations of reason, calling its integrity into question. As this process evolved, it became more difficult to identify, as Maupassant showed, the profile of fear. In *The Turn of the Screw*, the governess constantly finds herself unable to diagnose or name the apprehension she detects, "the strange, dizzy lift or swim (I try for terms!)," and yet, ultimately, fright does incarnate itself in the figures of the servants, whom the same governess calls "the outsiders."

A double and contradictory trend seemed, then, to shape the representation of unreason. On the one hand, monstrosity was perceived as an integral part of the self; on the other, monsters were portrayed as alien to bourgeois society. Such was the case in James's novel, but it must also be remembered that Dracula came from Transylvania and the Horla from Brazil—a fact that also denoted the new economic relations between Europe and the rest of the world. Unreason was, then, simultaneously a part of order and external to it, a contradiction which, as we shall see, was only apparent.[3]

Monster figures still maintained a certain relation to those sectors of society from which they had drawn their source of inspiration. *Dr. Jekyll and Mr. Hyde*, for instance, as the preface to the novel indicates, was based partly on the life of the famous Deacon Brodie, "the respectable artisan by day, a burglar at night." Furthermore, by dealing with alcoholism (Hyde was released by a drink) Stevenson was alluding to a problem considered an intrinsic condition of the lower classes.[4] The word *servants*, of course, referred directly to the working classes, and according to Tobias, "there is ample testimony . . . that domestic servants were often involved in criminal enterprises against their masters" (167). Beyond any discussion about the quantitative aspect of domestic servant criminality, what did take place, once again, was a qualitative change. As the century advanced, that particular economic sector underwent profound transformations. As domestic servants joined capitalist relations of production, they lost their status as "members of the family" to become workers inserted within the household structure.[5]

Thus, at the immediate level, the monsters of unreason could still be associated with that barbarism that threatened, from underneath, the stability of society. But, from an epistemological point of view, monstrosity definitely belonged to reason. The difficulties in profiling unreason were due to the intensification, in social awareness, of the internalization of this latter aspect. Balzac had noted, as had Marx and many others, the real terms of the paradox. Referring to the material conditions of existence, he asked in *Topographie médicale*: "Does it not seem that man is destined to find his destruction in the very causes of his existence?" (Chevalier, 384). By the end of the century, the search for unreason would lead inevitably to introspective pursuits. Marcel Schwob, in *Cœur double* (1891), would portray terror as being interior to man, provoked by man himself in his search for quintessential sensations, whether in love, in art, or in the uncanny experiences that could drive him to the beyond. Freud could, from these premises, develop a theoretical framework for the investigation of the unconscious—and of the fantastic, as he demonstrated in "Das Unheimlich."

The entire problem was summarized in Rimbaud's "Je est un autre." A crisis in representation was in the process of formation, a crisis that would explode at the turn of the century with the eruption of the entire spectrum of modernist movements. In a way, even the cultivation of physical appearance, the cult of the image that the "dandy" fervently embraced, could be understood in part as the effort to draw a contour of an identity plunged in conflict. For Anna Balakian, the decadent *gouffre* represents precisely a "frontier between the visible and the invisible, conscious and unconsciousness, life and nonlife" (70).

Stevenson's novel was also rooted in this crisis. Frankenstein projected his own otherness, reifying it in the monster in much the same way that Dr. Jekyll did in Mr. Hyde. In the latter, however, the relation of continuity between the two beings was no longer veiled: Jekyll and Hyde were, in effect, the same person. The duality of the character was openly exposed without the need to resort to figurative or psychoanalytic interpretations: "Though so profound a double-dealer, I was in no sense a hypocrite; both sides of me were in dead earnest; I was no more myself when I laid aside restraint and plunged in shame, than when I laboured, in the eye of the day, at the furtherance of knowledge or the relief of sorrow and suffering" (429). Jekyll's identity crisis assumed pathological proportions. With the disappearance of confinement, that social gesture and place which, as Foucault said, constituted "the separation of reason from unreason," madness ended up as a floating condition, useless as a measure of normality: "The romanticizing of madness reflects in the most vehement way the contemporary prestige of irrational or rude (spontaneous) behavior" (Sontag, 35). Indeed, the frontiers between artistic sensitivity and madness became an extremely elusive separation. Sanity and insanity lost their conceptual validity. For Maupassant, the madman was the only lucid being, the only one who could reach the limits of an indisputable truth. As he said in *Madame Hermet* (1887): "Madmen have a fascination for me. . . . For them, impossibility does not exist, *l'invraisemblable* disappears, the marvelous becomes constant and the supernatural turns familiar. Logic (that ancient barrier), reason (that ancient obstacle), and common sense (that ancient defense of the mind) break down, fall down, crumble away" (1976, 451). The premises of bourgeois epistemology appeared to be crumbling. If madness had been exiled during the classical age, during this new "age of materialism" it had returned, reinvaded society, and usurped the domain of reason.

3

Unreason had thus traveled the entire path, following a trajectory parallel to the one uncovered by Freud in his exploration of the concept of "the homely." A suppressed social category had come, with time, to resurface in order to occupy its opposite place of signification. In this sense *Dr. Jekyll and Mr. Hyde* articulated more than just a problem of absolute split identity. The two characters did not merely represent conflicting, opposing poles. On the contrary, Jekyll would always maintain a dominant role, showing to the world the multiplicity of his inner reality. His metamorphosis into Hyde was only an act of "liberation" in which part of his total personality was let loose—hence Hyde's smaller stature. However, Stevenson's novel switched the main focus of the problem by inserting this identity crisis within an evolutionary, that is, historical, approach. Hyde (and this is where the real innovation resided in relation to prior fantastic works) would ultimately replace Jekyll: "Hence, although I had now two characters as well as two appearances, one was wholly evil, and the other was still the old Henry Jekyll, that incongruous compound of whose reformation and improvement I had already learned to despair. The movement was thus wholly toward the worse" (435). The takeover by the forces of unreason was presented as inevitable.

Therefore, historical development pointed toward the irrevocable disappearance of dominant culture. Social evolution might eradicate the remnants of a primitive and barbarian past, but it also revealed, through its own postulates, the fragility of the bourgeois world and its eventual final transformation. The ambivalent reaction to science and progress that had formed part of nineteenth-century culture intensified at the turn of the twentieth century and in particular after World War I: "The war had destroyed both the notional neutrality of science, and the idea that the scientist was an unequivocally benevolent agent of social well-being. Instead, science seemed to many to be both 'Destroyer and Healer in One'" (MacLeod and MacLeod, 321). The concept of progress, then, that strong pillar of bourgeois epistemology, appeared to be called into question. A society that had used historical development as a means to justify its coming into power could, by the end of the nineteenth century, clearly see in that same principle the seeds for the destruction of its own universe. Maupassant lucidly laid out the terms of the conflict in *Le Horla*. First of all, projections into the future had to be acknowledged in a fantastic guise: "It is as if man, the thinker, has had a foreboding vision of some new being, mightier than himself, who shall succeed him in this world; and, in his terror, feeling him draw near, and unable to guess at the nature of his master, he has created all the fantastic crowd of occult beings, dim phantoms born of fear" (1925, 81–82).

As Rosemary Jackson points out, "The shadow on the edges of bourgeois culture is variously identified, as black, mad, primitive, criminal, socially deprived, deviant, crippled, or (when sexually assertive) female" (121). She also argues that, during the Victorian age, evil was basically assigned to very concrete figures, such as the worker/revolutionary, the foreigner, the madman, or the active woman. It is clear, then, that norms in fantastic literature (as in dominant ideology) were determined by the image of a bourgeois man. Any society organized around other premises had to be conceived of as abnormal and unnatural. The threat of a revolutionary workers' takeover, therefore, not only produced real fears but also fed, as Maupassant indicated, the representation of "unreal" or "supernatural" dangers. The Horla might be invisible, a void ready to adopt any suitable form, a "body-snatcher"; but there is no doubt that its mission is to usurp "man's" place on Earth and to destroy his society: "The Horla is going to make of man what we have made of the horse and the cow: his thing, his servant and his food" (1925, 85). The ideas of historical change and biological evolution fused into one single theory to which Maupassant appealed in suggesting a scientific authority for the concept of social metamorphosis: "A new being! why not? He must assuredly come! why should we be the last? . . . There have been so few kinds created in the world, from the bivalve to man. Why not one more, when we reach the end of the period of time that separates each successive appearance of a species from that which appeared before it?" (1925, 86–87). No order is permanent; the new reign of the monstrous is perfectly plausible; bourgeois civilization is not the culmination of historical development but just another link in the chain of evolution.

Faced with this eventuality, the solutions adopted by the bourgeoisie in order to negate its own idea of historical progress revealed, as the events of La Commune anticipated, the full extent of the crisis affecting dominant epistemology. In spite of recognizing the inevitability of the transformations he foresees, the protagonist in *Le Horla* decides to act and fight. The final result is in itself symbolic: he opts for burning down his house, servants included, and the tale ends with the premonitory words, "after man, the Horla . . . I must kill myself, now . . ." (1925, 92; ellipses appear in the French original). This apparently futile gesture of self-destruction emerged as the only alternative to the seriousness of the situation. To destroy order so as to preserve order: this was the paradox confronted by dominant society as the century came to an end. Such a suicidal attitude would later, in the 1920s and 1930s, find concrete political formulations in fascist programs and ideals. In the meantime, the dilemma the bourgeoisie had to deal with had not yet reached the moment of "the final solution." Jekyll-Hyde does commit suicide, but *Le Horla* ends with an ellipsis, as if there were still a possibility, a remote chance, of modifying the historical vision.

The last third of the nineteenth century witnessed profound transformations. At the ideological level, the liberal program had been institutionalized as a rational alternative to the irrational aspects of capitalism that created social injustice and, therefore, the material conditions for rebellion and subversion. After La Commune, the dominant political spectrum was polarized: "From the 1870's on," says Hobsbawm, "this virtual monopoly of the bourgeois programme (in its 'liberal' forms) began to crumble" (1975, 276). Class struggle, as Paris had demonstrated, required the acceptance of attitudes that could contradict the foundational rhetoric of the bourgeois state. Between 1871 and 1929, to use two symbolic dates, the ideological backbone of capitalism suffered a progressive disintegration: reason, the great instrument of bourgeois liberation, was now in the hands of the worker movements, and social development seemed to confirm all the projections ingrained in that discourse. Thus, little by little, dominant culture had to face the dilemma of either negating its own philosophical postulates or accepting that, in effect, a socialist universe would have to be constructed. Georg Lukács explored this situation in *The Destruction of Reason*: "Accordingly, the first important period of modern irrationalism has its origin in the struggle against the idealist dialectical-historical concept of progress. . . . With the June massacre of the Parisian proletariat and with the Paris Commune in particular, the situation altered quite radically. From that time onwards the proletariat's worldview, dialectical and historical materialism, was the adversary whose character determined the further development of irrationalism" (7). Reason, therefore, ceased to be a valid justification of order, and unreason dominated the horizon as the only possible alternative with which to defend the status quo. This epistemological exchange had necessarily to produce a crisis in language and signification—as Lewis Carroll, for instance, fully explored in his *Alice in Wonderland*. The fantastic was an appropriate vehicle not only for expressing this process but also for creating the ideological framework from which to negate the idea of progress and reject the old Cartesian principles.[6]

The ending in *Le Horla* suggests a need for the adoption of actions of an extraordinary nature, even if they challenge reasonable principles. For Hans Kohn, the first decades of the twentieth century saw the replacement of the outdated *cogito ergo sum* by the more pertinent *agitamus ergo sumus*. Reason suddenly became an antiquated and powerless instrument, and the old mechanisms of order, its social and legal institutions, became totally inefficient.[7] In Bram Stoker's *Dracula* (1897), the invasion of the vampire could not be checked with scientific instruments and had to be destroyed through the use of primitive, superstitious, unreasonable weapons: a cross, a garlic clove. In *The Turn of the Screw* the terms of the conflict were fully addressed and delineated.

In James's novel, the family structure plays a central role. As the process of internalization of threat advanced during the nineteenth century, the family—the house—became an adequate symbolic entity for the representation of tension. If, with the consolidation of the nuclear family, the home had assumed the function of a secure retreat, of a self-banished space that could protect the family from the problems of the outside, the articulation of internal danger would appropriate that same house as an effective metaphorical locus.[8] The family could easily condense the premises of society and depict moral and sexual aggressions, rebellions against authority, generational conflicts, and so on. In *The Turn of the Screw*, the family presents some peculiar characteristics, since both parents are dead and the education of the children is put under the supervision of a governess, a central character for the narrative but an outsider to the family makeup. The structure, then, upon which the action is constructed could be schematized in the following way: the uncle, the person in charge of the economic well-being of the family, has relinquished all domestic authority to the governess and will not intervene in the action; the governess accepts a position that, from the beginning and without concrete reasons, is presented as dangerous:

> "And what did the former governess die of?—of so much respectability?"
> Our friend's answer was prompt. "That will come out. I don't anticipate."
> "In her succesor's place," I suggested, "I should have wished to learn if the office brought with it—"
> "Necessary danger to life?" Douglas completed my thought.
>
> (8)

A series of servants, especially Mrs. Grose, collaborate passively with the governess; the monsters, two resuscitated ex-servants, create the tension with their apparitions; and the children, Flora and Miles, are trapped in the center of a struggle between the governess and the ex-servants to determine who will "possess" them. The ultimate question hovering over the story is, of course, whether the children will fall into darkness and be overtaken by the forces of unreason or whether, on the contrary, they will remain within the framework of family order.

The social projections of the conflict, then, seem clear, and a succession of transpositions could easily be formulated. Could the uncle figure not represent a high bourgeoisie unable, in a concrete historical moment, to assume the direct responsibilities of the future? Could the children not incarnate that bourgeois future? Were those monsters not the already too familiar figures of the working classes?

The monsters' challenge assumes in the text revolutionary proportions: "I [the governess] was by the strangest of chances wondering how I should meet him [Miles] when the revolution unmistakably occurred. I call it a revolution because I now see how, with the word he spoke, the curtain rose on the last act of my dreadful drama and the catastrophe was precipitated" (59). Miles's rebellion was not without reasons nor without objectives. The demonic forces might be blamed for the children's attitude, but what the boy demanded had specific connotations and was very much a part of this world. He claimed, in fact, a right that formed part of the bourgeois discourse—liberty: "[Miles] had got out of me that there was something I was much afraid of and that he should probably be able to make use of my fear to gain for his own purpose, more freedom" (62). The same principles of liberty that had been used a century before to dismantle the ancien régime appeared now to challenge the institutions of order embodied by the governess. Dr. Jekyll, in his moments of lucidity, would approach the same issue: "Yes, I preferred the elderly and discontented doctor, surrounded by friends and cherishing honest hopes; and bade a resolute farewell to the liberty, the comparative youth, the light step, leaping impulses and secret pleasures, that I had enjoyed in the disguise of Hyde" (442).

The situation, then, that the governess had to confront was indeed extraordinary, and the measures she would have to adopt in order to fight the emancipatory claims would also need to be extraordinary. The characteristics of the conflict did not allow for respectable and rational behavior; action (as Kohn affirmed when proposing *agitamus ergo sumus* as the fin de siècle motto) was the required immediate response: "Yet I believe that no woman so overwhelmed ever in so short a time recovered her command of the act" (James, 91). Such an "act" would consist of keeping "the boy himself unaware," of depoliticizing him—but it would eventually require more drastic measures. In the final scene of *The Turn of the Screw*, the governess "kills" young Miles and thus creates a confusion as to who the real monster is. This unreasonable act becomes the final logical response to the menace posed to the house, of whose well-being and proper conduct the governess is in charge: "Here at present I felt afresh—for I had felt it again

97

and again—how my equilibrium depended on the success of my rigid will, the will to shut my eyes as tight as possible to the truth that what I had to deal with was, revoltingly, against nature. I could only get on at all by taking 'nature' into my confidence and my account, by treating my monstrous ordeal as a push in a direction unusual, of course, and unpleasant, but demanding, after all, for a fair front, only another turn of the screw of ordinary human virtue" (86).

The governess won the battle through the use of radical measures. But the solution fell completely within the domain of unreason. Reason proved to be inadequate in dealing with new historical situations, while extraordinary and even criminal actions were rationalized as a necessary extension of normal values. Miles, as Muriel West demonstrates, was executed. With the death of the child, the monsters also disappeared. Thus Maupassant's ellipsis found, in a way, an answer: in effect, self-destruction could eliminate the dangers ingrained in progress, in historical development. It was a solution, nevertheless, that implied the transformation of the ideological premises that sustained the economic system. It implied the abandonment of reason as the epistemological foundation of bourgeois order and the acceptance of unreason as a "natural" premise.

4

A central, crucial paradox, therefore, dominated the cultural panorama at the turn of the twentieth century: the discourse of reason that had served to promote and justify the ascent of the bourgeois world now articulated its own negation. The premises of that discourse were used precisely by that sector that had been excluded from the rational world to build an alternative society. The discourse of reason would shape the voice of the working class; unreason, on the other hand, would be adopted by the dominant sector precisely and paradoxically as a means of avoiding the collapse of order. Bourgeois epistemology, immersed in this exchange, was left floating in a universe apparently without meaning. The fantastic abandoned its confining frame and invaded the entire cultural landscape, bringing its representation of paradox, of antinomy, to all corners of artistic activity.

Unreason was present everywhere; emptiness had no form, but was capable of assuming them all; meaning seemed to be inapprehensible . . . how could otherness be distinguished from the self? "Thus we imperceptibly move from the description of perversities and oddities to the description of uncanny events presented as emblematic occurrences of a society. . . . Distortion and the impossibility of clearly locating the Self are at the origins of the literature of the uncanny that flourished between 1880 and 1900. The boundaries between life and death, between the world and internal life, became too blurred for the universe to make sense" (Bancquart, xxiii–xxiv). By eliminating the frontiers between the self and the other, between subject and object, art tended to abandon the idea that it was representation, that it stood in relation to an objective reality, that its transformation of the material world needed to incorporate a referential sense. "Distortion," says Lukács in "The Ideology of Modernism," "becomes as inseparable a part of the portrayal of reality as the recourse to the pathological. But literature must have a concept of the normal if it is to place distortion correctly, that is to say, to see it as distortion" (1973, 293). Gradually, art acquired an autonomy that "liberated" it from its relation with reality. The frontiers separating the reflected image from its referent would be put into question. Thus, for instance, when Klee said that the world in its actual form was not the only possible world, he was referring to all the other worlds that the artist could detect or even invent, "and invention, here, meant another unconscious method of detecting the invisible" (Brion, 171). As Brion continues, the function of the artist became to expose this unseen world anticipated by him. Once again, however, reality could only be understood as deceit, since it showed an appearance that hid another and equally valid dimension.[9]

In *Le Horla* the mirror plays an important role. As Bancquart shows, it generates fear by blurring and questioning the limits separating the self from the other; but it also serves as a door to other systems, with other rules, that can reveal a true nature in reality not suspected or permitted by the accepted laws governing the universe. A mirror would allow the protagonist to confirm the existence of the invisible being: "The room was as light as day, and I could not see myself in my looking-glass! It was empty, transparent, deep, filled with light! I was not reflected in it. . . . And I stared at it with a distraught gaze: I daren't move another step, I daren't make another movement; nevertheless I felt he was there, whose immaterial body had swallowed up my reflection, but that he would elude me still" (1925, 88).

This double character of the mirror (autonomous world yet, at the same time, unveiling instrument of the restrictions imposed on reality) of course affected all types of cultural production. Paintings acquired a life of their own in M. R. James's stories; Oscar Wilde would say in *De profundis* that nature was, as life, an imitation of art, and Dorian Gray would manage to stop time, to stop historical development, by making his portrait suffer the physical changes of aging. In other words, fantastic art and the avant-garde would share the same basic principles, making it almost impossible to separate them. Starting with the twentieth century, the analysis of the fantastic requires the study of the central cultural expressions of modernism.

Unreason became a quotidian magic, an ordinary occurrence in which the natural and the supernatural appeared at the same level, hence forgoing any claims to representation and ultimately to meaning. Thus, for instance, in Franz Kafka's *The Metamorphosis* Gregor Samsa's "unreal" transformation is decisively offered as unremarkably "real." But the fantastic remained an expression of fugacity, an articulation of the tensions provoked by historical development. Renato Poggioli's assertions about the avant-garde could also be applied to the fantastic as part of its historical characterization: "The sense or consciousness of belonging to an intermediate stage, to a present already distinct from the past and to a future in potentiality which will be valid only when the future is actuality, all this explains the origin of the idea of transition, that agonistic concept par excellence, favorite myth of an apocalyptic and crisis-ridden era, a myth particularly dear to the most recent avant-gardes" (72).

All this, of course, must be perceived within a broader panorama in which social relations had in effect suffered profound changes and assumed a configuration very different from in previous epochs. The process of transformation that the dual revolution had inaugurated in Europe accelerated at the end of the nineteenth century. From political changes (the Soviet Revolution) to the fast succession of inventions and technological discoveries, reality did indeed seem to decompose under the eyes of contemporary men and women.[10] For Baronian, this situation was determinate in Maupassant's writings: "His fantastic is that—only that: the objective expression of the decomposition of evidence" (122).

The disintegration of reality opened up the possibility of conceiving numerous realities, more or less visible but all with the same right to existence. The problem had already been noted by Dr. Jekyll: "Man is not truly one, but truly two. I say two, because the state of my own knowledge does not pass beyond that point. Others will follow . . . and I hazard the guess that man will be ultimately known for a mere polity of multifarious, incongruous, and independent denizens" (429). Jekyll's proposal could be extended to all levels of reality. For Oscar Wilde, in De profundis, "time and space, succession and extension, are merely accidental conditions of thought. The Imagination can transcend them, and move in a free sphere of ideal existences. Things, also, are in their essence what we choose to make them. A thing is, according to the mode in

101

which one looks at it" (187). Even though in *De profundis* Wilde asserted that he had found meaning, his idealist position implied that all the coordinates of reality were arbitrary. Just as Baudelaire had anticipated, the only alternative was to renounce the possibility of apprehending it. Thus, unreason was no longer limited to a periphery or to an alternative to order; unreason became reality and thus could reside in the most ordinary and common object, since the differentiation between it and the powerful rule of reason was null: "There is a familiar sentiment of mystery felt for those things that we agree to qualify as mysterious; but the supreme sentiment is the nonfamiliar sentiment of mystery felt for those things that we agree to find natural, familiar" (Brion, 278).

Unreason, internalized on the one hand, unrecognizable on the other, perhaps present under the most ordinary aspects (forms) of everyday life, was la Nada, the vacuum—and therefore plenitude as well. Unreason lost its place, its identification, its name. The formulation of unreason, a search for a language that could express it, would become the new paradox of the fantastic: the discovery of a system of representation that could project meaning in its nonmeaning, that could demonstrate the absurdity of representation through representation, that could justify the reasonable foundations of unreason. The formalization of antinomy, then, became the central concern of fantastic art. Discourse itself provided the space in which to attempt to reduce epistemological uncertainty. Such is, for instance, the basic tension experienced between the "supernatural" events presented in Kafka's *The Metamorphosis* and the meticulous, "realistic and natural" language that gives them form.[11] The formalization of the premises of fantastic art was, undoubtedly, a necessary step in the preservation of socioeconomic dominance, since the efficient pursuit of economic performance required a rational/reasonable and scientific approach to material production and an irrational/unreasonable formulation of human existence. Horkheimer presents it clearly:

The human being, in the process of his emancipation, shares the fate of the rest of his world. Domination of nature involves domination of man. Each subject not only has to take part in the subjugation of external nature, human and non-human, but in order to do so must subjugate nature in himself. Domination becomes 'internalized' for dominion's sake. What is usually indicated as a goal—the happiness of the individual, health, and wealth—gains its significance exclusively from its functional potentiality. These terms designate favorable conditions for intellectual and material production. Therefore self-renunciation of the individual in industrialist society has no goal transcending industrialist society. *Such abnegation brings about rationality with reference to means and irrationality with reference to human existence.* . . . Resistance and revulsion arising from this repression of nature have beset civilization from its beginnings, in the form of social rebellions . . . as well as in the form of individual crime and mental derangement. Typical of our present era is the manipulation of this revolt. . . . Civilization as rationalized irrationality integrates the revolt of nature as another means or instrument. (93–94; emphasis mine)

By the 1900s the fantastic had ceased to be the shadow of realism to become the new central element of artistic expression. In *Dracula* Dr. Van Helsing gives to Dr. Seward a concise explanation of the perception held by dominant culture at the end of the century: "You deal with the madmen. All men are mad in some way or the other; and inasmuch as you deal discreetly with your madmen, so deal with God's madmen, too—the rest of the world" (114). The eclipse of reason followed a long trajectory shaped by and expressed through the fantastic. At the turn of the twentieth century, unreason finally broke its chains of confinement and extended its presence across the entire social landscape.

103

|||| FIVE |||||

Shadows

1

SPAIN'S historical development presents fundamental differences from the major political and economic trends that affected other European countries, particularly France and England. By the eighteenth century, the "backwardness" of Spanish society had become an irrefutable fact, and the Peninsula lay at the periphery of Europe, in the shadows of the northern economic powers. The consolidation of the bourgeois state and the formation of a hegemonic bourgeois ideology would occur much later, during the second half of the nineteenth century.

In spite of the fact that profound differences separated Spain and Germany, the development of the two countries coincided in several respects, especially in those pertaining to their political formation. Thus, Georg Lukács's analysis in *The Historical Novel* of the German situation could very well be applied to Spain:

> In England and France, the economic, political and ideological preparation and completion of the bourgeois revolution and the setting-up of a national state are one and the same process. So that in looking to the past, however intense the bourgeois-revolutionary patriotism and however important the works it produces (Voltaire's *Henriade*), the chief concern is inevitably the Enlightenment critique of the "unreasonable." Not so in Germany. Here revolutionary patriotism comes up against national division, against the political and economic fragmentation of a country which imports its cultural and ideological means of expression from France. . . . The German form of Enlightenment necessarily engages in sharp polemic with this French culture;

and it preserves this note of revolutionary patriotism even when the real content of the ideological battle is simply the conflict between different stages in the development of the Enlightenment. . . . The inevitable result of this situation is to turn to German history. Partly it is the reawakening of past national greatness which gives strength to hopes of national rebirth. (22)

Spain confronted a similar situation, at least in regard to the gap existing between the appearance of an enlightened political program and the consolidation of the modern nation-state. Enlightenment came through the Bourbon dynasty, in particular through Charles III, who tried to modernize the country from above—an initiative that immediately encountered serious opposition from dominant sectors of Spanish society. Since its inception, the enlightened agenda was identified with the royal program. This association, then, between Enlightenment and the French dynasty would weigh in the subsequent development of bourgeois consciousness during the nineteenth century, since the establishment of bourgeois revolutionary patriotism would find political difficulties in reconciling "foreign" postulates with its own national program. This inherent tension in the gestation of Spanish middle-class ideology assumed critical proportions, as we have seen apropos of Goya, after the invasion of the Peninsula by Napoleon's troops.[1]

If the progressive measures taken by Charles III had served, paradoxically, to hinder the growth of a bourgeois consciousness, the truly reactionary measures undertaken by his successor, Charles IV, generated the opposite trend. Gradually, the Spanish bourgeoisie realized that it shared fundamental principles with the French bourgeoisie, and the criticism directed at the *afrancesados* diminished, until the war with France cast a fatal blow to the final consolidation of an ideology akin to the Enlightenment.[2] From this situation, the ascent of the middle class bore the stigma of having to create its ideological framework, emphasizing different principles from those embraced in England or France; its self-affirmation would be built not in opposition to an "unreasonable" past but rather in accordance with it, drawing from history those elements that could serve to justify and enhance national middle-class values.[3] In addition, the loss of the American colonies served to intensify the trend for the "reawakening of past national greatness," to use Lukács's words.

The return of Ferdinand VII to power, especially after the self-inflicted coup of 1823 that reinstalled an absolute monarchy, produced the conditions that allowed for the emergence and ultimate formation of a hegemonic bourgeois ideology. The "ominous decade" in which the king ruled despotically and arbitrarily made it clear that a modern and powerful Spain had to discard and eliminate its feudal structures. Drastic changes were needed in order to redress the economic "backwardness" and dependence of the country.[4] Nevertheless, the Spanish bourgeoisie was forced to exercise moderation in the execution of such changes, since throughout the first part of the nineteenth century threats to the implementation of the new order came not only from below but also from above, from the entrenched forces of feudalism incarnated in Carlism. This moderation was also dictated by the historical precedents of the revolutionary waves that had shaken Europe, including Spain, at the turn of the century. The revolution of 1792 in France, or the Cadiz Constitution of 1812, clearly marked the limits of the reforms that the bourgeoisie was ready to implement. Eugenio de Ochoa, for instance—one of the first Spanish authors to attempt to write fantastic stories[5]—openly addressed, in the first issue of *El artista*, the fears that the events of Paris had generated: "We know that in all countries revolutions are slowly spreading their underground tunnels—ramifications of the great central revolution whose focal point is the French capital" (3).

Without any doubt, then, Spain's late development created specific conditions that had a decisive influence on the formation of its dominant ideology—and, therefore, of its literary production. Cultural and economic dependence played an important role, as can be confirmed not only by the number of translations that invaded the Peninsula or by the zeal to imitate and "import" trends, but also by the fact that such a phenomenon was imprinted over the cultural needs and tastes of Spanish society, thus helping to shape, in part, the hybrid literary situation of the first half of the nineteenth century. On the one hand, the years between 1830 and 1860 are generally considered to constitute the period in which romanticism flourished in Spain, a fact that will lead to talk of a postromantic or second romantic movement when dealing with the works of Gustavo Adolfo Bécquer. And yet on the other hand, this is precisely the period during which the bourgeoisie promoted an entire program of ideological and cultural definitions that, in a sense, functioned in much the same way as the writings of *les philosophes* had in France.[6] *Costumbrismo*, for example, was a genre that arose and expanded through the press[7] in order to educate and to foment the values of the bourgeoisie, values that included a new concept of nation—a centralized and unified Spain portrayed through the life of Madrid—and the depiction of the reasonable and just habits of the middle class. As Susan Kirkpatrick indicates, "with conscious conviction, Mesonero represents the habits, styles, dilemmas, speech and activities of Madrid's bourgeoisie and petite bourgeoisie as the image of Spanish social life, as 'naturaleza . . . revestida de forma española.' His *Cuadros de costumbre* appropriate the myth of 'nation' for the bourgeoisie, making in effect the ideological statement that the emerging bourgeois life-style and values constitute the natural, national character of Spain" (33–34).

The first half of the nineteenth century, then, witnessed, especially after the death of Ferdinand VII in 1833, the rise of a new Spain that projected through genres such as costumbrismo the "ideological manifestation of the transition to modern, bourgeois society" (Kirkpatrick, 31). At the same time that this process was taking place, at the same time that the foundations of the new "reasonable" nation were being erected, romanticism burst onto the scene, incorporating many of the characteristics and problems that corresponded not to the transitional phase of the formation of the bourgeois state, but rather to its period of consolidation. This coexistence of two cultural currents belonging to different developmental stages must be taken into account if we are to delimit the framework of the fantastic in Spain. I will postulate that, in spite of the fact that numerous legends and tales—most of them in verse—of the supernatural were published in Spain before 1850, a corpus of fantastic literature did not appear and was not established until Bécquer wrote his legends at the beginning of the second half of the nineteenth century. This does not imply that Bécquer represents an absolute break, a radical shift in cultural development. There existed some "true" fantastic precedents, such as the works of Eugenio de Ochoa or some of Gertrudis Gómez de Avellaneda's short stories. But these are either isolated cases within the dominant trend (cases that would reflect the complexity of the phenomenon of cultural and economic dependence) or works that need to be examined more in depth in order to determine their exact nature. Thus, for instance, Clark Gallaher considers that two of Avellaneda's stories, *La flor del ángel* and *El aura blanca, suceso extraño ocurrido en nuestros días*, though containing "unearthly elements, are really Christian mysteries rather than fantastic tales" (20). For Rafael Llopis, who equates the fantastic with romanticism, the first decades of the century offered only sacred literature, since the "element of skepticism required by the fantastic was not yet present in Spanish society" (94).

A first appraisal of the impressions and judgments of modern critics reveals a general consensus in recognizing Bécquer's legends as different from previous ones—in a sense, as a "new species," to recall Walter Scott's phrase in regard to *Otranto*.[8] The supernatural stories written in Spain prior to Bécquer were also regarded by contemporaries as distinct from the foreign tales that reached the country: "They agreed with Raphael in *La gaviota* that 'this is good for you Germans; not for us. A Spanish fantastic novel would be an insupportable affectation'." (Gallaher, 3). The belief that the fantastic was something "different" from what was being produced in the Peninsula appears clearly reflected in the following anecdote related to the publication, in 1847, of a translation of a collection of short stories by E.T.A. Hoffmann: "It was this book evidently that Zorrilla's wife was reading one day when she suggested to him that he write a tale in the style of Hoffmann. But he countered that in a country like theirs, 'full of light and life, whose inhabitants live in the arms of the most complete idleness, without taking the trouble of trying to obtain more happiness than the inappreciable one of having been born Spaniards, who would chase through those realms of space after the phantoms, apparitions, gnomes, and giants of that silly German?'" (Gallaher, 5).[9] But, as Zorrilla's wife pointed out, he had already written works that included apparitions and phantoms, a contradiction that indicated the extent to which the Spanish supernatural of the time was perceived as different.[10] For Gallaher, in spite of the fact that his article is an attempt to establish a continuity between Bécquer's work and a previous tradition, there is also a clear difference between writers of the romantic movement and those publishing during the years more closely preceding Bécquer, although he attributes the difference to the author's skill and not to the characteristics of the works. While no definitions are given for the fantastic, Gallaher's remarks are conclusive: "In spite of all this accumulated evidence of supernatural forces at work in Spanish literature, few fantastic tales were produced during the culmination of the romantic movement. . . . Its men of letters turned to the poetic legend when they delved in the supernatural" (8).

All these examples, then, serve to trace a formal or generic as well as historical separation between two types of tales. Thus, the emergence of a Spanish fantastic production can only be recorded starting in the decade of the fifties, namely, after the consolidation of a bourgeois society. It is not, therefore, surprising that the tales classified by Baquero Goyanes as fantastic are dated after 1840 and belong, for the most part, to the second half of the nineteenth century—a fact also verified by Antonio Risco.[11] Risco, who follows Todorov's premises very closely, does not specify why he does not take into account the extensive literary production of the first half of the century that dealt with the supernatural. Nevertheless, he is also implicitly affirming both a generic and a historical distinction, making Bécquer, for all intents and purposes, the first significant representative of the fantastic.[12]

Given the present state of research on the Spanish fantastic, a more exhaustive study of that "legendary" production of the first part of the century would be needed in order to determine the basic traits that define it—both by itself and in relation to fantastic literature in general. Nevertheless, some general and preliminary conclusions can be suggested. During that period, one of the basic problems facing the Spanish bourgeoisie was the need to elaborate a program that could assert the ideas of progress and tradition simultaneously. Progress was deemed essential insofar as the new middle classes perceived the need to transform the feudal and anachronic structures that still dominated Spanish society; land disentailment became, until 1857, the single most important political, social, and economic issue of the first part of the century.[13] Tradition was valued insofar as the patriotic principles upon which to build the new modern nation, at this stage, could no longer be based on the premises defended by the Enlightenment; the efforts to erect the new society were, then, based upon exalting a glorious national past. This double proposition could in principle accommodate, after the death of Ferdinand VII in 1833, all the sectors of the dominant classes, with the exception of the Carlists, who defended the most traditional worldview and economic organization.

The result was that the selection of values implied in the elaboration of a tradition through legends and historical novels tended to attack the absolute and arbitrary power attributed to feudal societies—a characteristic, one must not forget, embodied in the Carlist threat—and, simultaneously, enhance the vision of an organic world, united and harmoniously ruled by the sacred laws of God. *Romances*, traditions, short stories, and novels set in the Middle Ages emphasized different aspects of, for instance, the Reconquista in order to highlight the existence of a Spanish essence based on its deep Christian commitment and on a common national origin. The vast majority of these works were moralistic or didactic, offering to the modern reader some universal and ahistorical traits of the Spanish national character.[14] From this perspective, then, the romantic historical novel of the first half of the nineteenth century, as well as the legend or the "traditional" short story, functioned in a similar way as costumbrismo.[15] They all collaborated in affirming those transcendental values needed to consolidate the oligarchy and the middle classes in their leading role in the emerging new Spain.

To reconcile progress with tradition—such was the task undertaken by the dominant sectors of Spain during the formative years of the bourgeois society. In the depiction of contemporary Spain, then, the historical past portrayed in this early nineteenth century literature operated not in opposition to the present, as had been the case, for instance, in *Otranto*, but in conjunction with it. Supernatural events appeared not as a source of tension, not as a means of questioning nature, but as part of nature. They might be supernatural, but they were not unnatural. The fundamental characteristics of a Gothic literature were not, therefore, attained. Only after 1860 could a production with Gothic elements emerge in Spain, a literature in which the past was not appropriated as a source of harmonizing values, but discovered as the witness of historical evolution. The past would then become an antagonistic space, a fracture within the by now consolidated bourgeois ideology. Thus, when José Pastor de la Roca published, in 1863, his collection of legends related to the palace of Villena, he could affirm that he was going to write "those fairy tales that nobody had dared to write yet" (Baquero 1949, 217). They were, in effect, "a new species of romance": "We shall evoke those light shadows that

111

sleep in unknown tunnels, and that, at the echo of those grotesque formulas of exorcism and under the cabalistic sign
drawn by the magic wand of the necromancer, will reveal to us
without resistance curious and somber mysteries that lie for-
gotten" (quoted by Baquero 1949, 217).

In general terms, then, the period between 1830 and 1860
must be considered as the Spanish version of the prerevolu-
tionary bourgeois epoch. During these years, the formation of
a new modern oligarchy that incorporated a bourgeois worldview required the abolition of feudal institutions and the accommodation of more efficient relations of production, a process that generated strains reminiscent of those experienced,
for instance, by France during the eighteenth century. The
long and often traumatic ascent of a "reasonable" Spanish society finally culminated in the mid–nineteenth century.[16] But the
triumph of reason immediately brought to the forefront new
problems: a replica of the Luddite movement appeared in the
1850s;[17] general riots broke out in 1854; revolution attempts
finally occurred in 1868. Undoubtedly, the intrusion of capitalist practices and of industrialization created appropriate conditions for the emergence of tensions that could be articulated
"in a fantastic guise." Furthermore, when alluding to a second,
or even third, romantic movement, critics are ultimately referring to the appearance of a national cultural current in accordance with the developmental stage of the country. From 1860
onward, Spain began to share the general European problems.
By the end of the century, in spite of all the differences in economic and political development, Spain had narrowed the gap
that separated her from Europe. Thus, when examining the
fantastic production of this second half of the nineteenth century, we can apply the paradigm established in the previous
chapters to the Spanish evolution. The Spanish fantastic portrayed a "Gothic" experience in which reason projected in the
past disturbing dreams about the future, followed almost immediately by periods of doubt about and negation of the idea
of progress—that concept that the same bourgeoisie had tried

to consolidate, with great difficulty, during the first half of the century.

2

Gustavo Adolfo Bécquer's *Legends*, emerging out of a cultural tradition that tinged the first half of the nineteenth century, were, then, a new kind of narrative.[18] This does not of course imply that there were no precedents. It does indicate, however, that with Bécquer an original literature, fully embodying a Gothic problem, appeared on the Spanish cultural horizon.[19] In a sense, Bécquer stood at the culmination of one process and at the beginning of a new one. He closed the period during which the bourgeoisie had struggled to impose a new world-view and, simultaneously, opened the shadows that this same vision projected toward the future. This pivotal position occupied by Bécquer, an author claimed by both tradition and modernity, may be the root of the difficulty encountered by critics in classifying him. As Rubén Benítez points out, "while by his esoteric language Bécquer proves his romantic origin, he also coincides with certain postromantic French authors in his search and appreciation of mystery. Like them, he has moved from the picturesque description characteristic of romanticism to the drawing of a 'forêt de symboles' where the sensations and objective world of the stone fuse into a unique and quivering desire of infinity" (57). Bécquer's work is presented as dominated by light and shade; elusive, nostalgic, and innovative; pagan and Christian. This contradictory character must be understood as a central motif in Bécquer's production, as a central paradox in his poetic formulation.

Antonio Risco's formal analysis of the *Legends* arrives at some interesting conclusions. According to Risco, the majority of the legends manifest a "vision that recognizes the intrusion of the supernatural in the real world . . . [and] they show a confusion between dream and reality" (57). By "real" must be understood a rational world in which reality is ruled by "objective" laws, a world in which the appearance of events that contradict these laws must necessarily provoke an intrusion. Accordingly, Benítez finds that "in all the cases, [the narrator's figure] thus created tends to smile with skepticism at the supernatural quality of the events, in the same way that did the readers of newspapers in a bourgeois and positivist century" (198).

Bécquer, without any doubt, was very conscious of the medium in which his legends were published. The introduction to *The Mountain of the Spirits* (*El monte de las Ánimas*) directly alludes to this problem: "At noon, after a good breakfast and smoking a cigar, [the story] will not have much effect on the readers of *El contemporáneo*. I heard it in the same place where it occurred, and I wrote it turning sometimes my head with fear when I heard the glass of my balcony crackle by the effects of the cold air of the night" (136). Just as Goya had excluded unreason from the Puerta del Sol at noon, Bécquer devised a space in which to portray the appearance of threats: they would not happen within the prosaic and material world embodied by the periodical. And yet it was in *El contemporáneo* where the story was published and read, thus reproducing the same paradox of representation articulated in *Los Caprichos*. Bécquer's legends, as Risco indicates, were all framed by introductions "that tend to estrange the narrated events, to register their abnormality, to exile the implicit reader outside of his daily world, rendering useless any attempt at believing in the imaginary events" (60). Risco concludes that "the enunciative situation of these legends tends to impose, then, a resultant realistic perspective and, therefore, a skeptical relation with the anecdote" (64). If Goya's actual depiction of the impossible monsters constituted the basis of the fantastic, Bécquer's "intrusion" into the reasonable society, by virtue of being acknowledged and enunciated as an intrusion, formulated the same dilemma. A fracture was established between reality and the supernatural; such an act was a clear recognition of the "reasonable" premises that sustained society. Once the triumph of reason had been accomplished, unreason could be acknowledged only as belonging to past beliefs that were no longer valid. Thus, in *The Devil's Cross* (*La cruz del diablo*) the cross is portrayed as "silent and simple expression of the beliefs and piety of other centuries" (105), and in *The Gold Bracelet* (*La ajorca de oro*) "he was superstitious and brave like all the men of his time" (127).

Bécquer's formulation of a dichotomy between context and text depicted a new problem. According to Baquero Goyanes, "Faith, the national bond, breaks down, and in its place emerges doubt, 'that sinister spirit of the nineteenth century that disturbs the mind and throws it into the dark abyss of German philosophy . . .' according to an ironic expression by Palacio Valdés" (305). Hence, beginning in the second half of the nineteenth century, the bourgeoisie found itself in a radically different position. Until that moment, it had had to carve its space in opposition to an entrenched dominant class that defended the economic organization and the prerogatives of the ancien régime; after that date the relation in the political composition of the country changed, giving the bourgeoisie a clearly dominant role within a newly formed oligarchy.[20] Within this framework, then, Bécquer articulated a situation similar to the one registered by Gothic literature: when reason seemed to have finally overcome a history of frustrations and setbacks, when it had finally secluded the last remnants of the old feudal society, unreason reappeared. And it reappeared following the same patterns erected by the Gothic. Unreason emerged from the margins, from the periphery of the social and cultural horizon. It emerged as a classification, contained within spaces of confinement: "In its [the Cathedral of Toledo's] bosom live silence, grandeur, mystic poetry and a holy horror that defends its threshold from worldly thoughts and earthly wretched passions. Material consumption can be alleviated by breathing the pure air of the mountains; atheism must be cured breathing its atmosphere of faith" (Bécquer, 131). Defying the material world of this new "prosaic century," the cathedral protected a universe appropriate not only for religious observance but also for the eruption of an ill-defined horror, a universe in which the laws that ruled "our" world could be violated. Thus, for instance, it was within a church that the statue of Doña Elvira could become alive in *The Kiss* (*El beso*). From this perspective, Bécquer's *History of the Temples of Spain* (*Historia de los templos de España*), his first major work, must be understood precisely as an effort to explore, discover, and create an inventory of the centers of confinement spread throughout the Peninsula.

But confinement was not the only setting for the supernatural. The vast majority of Bécquer's legends and tales articulate the notion of marginality. They take place in other times, generally the Middle Ages, or occasionally in other countries such as India. In fact, this feature was not limited to Bécquer; the majority of the literary production that during those years approached the fantastic generally located the narration in foreign countries—Germany, in particular, as Russell Sebold indicates, was very much in fashion during the sixties (39).[21] In *Hilda, a Fantastic Tale* (1867), Eugenio de Ochoa states it clearly: "The country of mysterious adventures, the fatherland of Sylphs and Undines, the predilect land of wizards and magicians, is Germany, the poetic, nebulous Germany. Its forests, as old as the earth and as dark as hell, are the refuge of innumerable goblins and phantoms" (Baquero 1949, 239).

It is, however, in the way in which Bécquer approached the past that the central premises of the Gothic appeared: he projected toward the past tensions foreseen in the future. Bécquer possessed a profound sense of historical development, of progress. History was assumed to be a series of connected events in which past, present and future formed links, stages of a coherent unity. In *Case of Ablative* (*Caso de ablativo*) he defined the Middle Ages as the prologue to "that giant poem that humanity has slowly developed through centuries. That is probably why I find a kind of secret relation between this last word of our civilization [the railroad] and those ancient towers [of the Burgos Cathedral]" (1043). Progress, in spite of Bécquer's con-

servative political convictions, was not acknowledged in order
to be negated. On the contrary, as Bécquer affirmed in "Letter
IV" of his *From My Cell* (*Desde mi celda*), "I have faith in the
future. New ideas are opening up new possibilities and destroying old barriers. The nineteenth century, like the Supreme
Creator in Genesis, can believe without vanity when contem-
plating its deed, that it was good" (1048). Thus Bécquer's
reevaluation of the past did not imply a longing for the medieval world: "This is not to say that I wish for me or anybody
else a return to those times. What was has no reason of being
again—and it will not be" (580). The fundamental problem resided, then, in reconciling, both aesthetically and ideologically,
his support of progress with his constant portrayal of a lost and
admired feudal world. For Rubén Benítez this dichotomy represents an inherent ideological contradiction that must be understood by taking into account the possible influence of Bal-
lanche and Lamenais: "The ideal resides not in a return to the
past but in the future of men united in a perfect society of religious content" (16).[22] However, that vision of a future was not
assumed by Bécquer in idealistic—nor even in optimistic—
terms.

When Bécquer affirmed that a "secret relation" threaded historical events into one single "gigantic poem," he was basically
suggesting that the passage of time was endowed with some
sort of meaning, albeit an unknown meaning. He was not, of
course, referring to the concept of evolution in the strict sense
of the word, since the intervention of God in the formation of
the "poem" was still determinate, but he nevertheless accepted
without hesitation the idea of historical concatenation: "The
day will come when the philosopher, once the broken links of
the chain are welded, will be able to unveil the marvelous and
uninterrupted unity of development that has taken us, with the
help of the Christian idea, from the cathedral to the locomotive
and from the locomotive to who knows where" (1043–44). For
Bécquer, history became, therefore, a text whose deciphering
could shed some light on the nature of that secret relation and

allow a projection toward the future. His *History of the Temples of Spain*, then, must be seen as a fundamental work from which Bécquer would develop his entire poetics: it is not merely an inventory of the existing places of confinement but also a catalogue of the historical signs that populated the Spanish landscape, a catalogue whose analysis could provide the needed clue to a vision of what lay ahead.

What Bécquer found written on the walls of those temples was not reassuring. On the one hand, it was true, their permanence attested to the survival of the pillars of a certain Spanish Christian tradition; on the other hand, a constant characteristic stood out: their ruinous state. The physical decadence of these buildings served as the concrete verification of the effects of time upon civilization. The new ideas, Bécquer stated in "Letter IV," had fatally wounded the old ones. Such an affirmation necessarily had to produce a fundamental questioning of the universal and eternal attributes of contemporary civilization: "Tomorrow, those who will come after us will see everything constituted in a different fashion and they will know that what existed a few centuries ago no longer exists; and they will ask themselves about the ways in which their parents lived; and nobody will have an answer" (584). Progress had made possible the "good" deed of the nineteenth century; by the same token, progress would end it. Ruins became, then, one of Bécquer's central artistic subjects, for they embodied the inevitability of change. In *Three Dates* (*Tres fechas*), for instance, the comparison between a ruinous plaza in Toledo and the surrounding buildings ultimately located artistic expression in the ruins. Thus nature by itself, insofar as it offered durability, immutability, or at most a cyclical pattern of repetition, was not the central focus of Bécquer's production. It acquired importance when it entered the domain of human creations, underlining either the ephemeral character of civilization or the inherent transformative quality of progress: nature could invade old buildings and monuments, or nature could be subverted by the implacable advance of the locomotive. It was at this tangent between two opposing realms that conflict could best be articulated. Thus when Bécquer found himself in places like Roncesvalles, completely dominated by nature and where no evidence of his central temporal concern could be located physically, he internalized the issue: "It is true that nothing of what surrounds us has changed here; but we have changed, I have changed" (1055).[23] Architecture became for Bécquer a constant motif, a preferred space of representation, because in it he could measure the effects of history.

Thus Bécquer's continual treatment of the past was not due to escapism, nor to a desire to relive an aristocratic world, but rather responded to a profound concern about the transformations projected into the future—transformations that were effected by the passage of time and embodied in the image of ruins. But change in itself, in abstract terms, did not suffice as a reason to question progress and accept decadence. The roots of concern resided in specific social conditions. In *Charity (Caridad)* Bécquer used a cholera outbreak to unveil the state of misery in which the inhabitants of Madrid lived, a situation that needed to be solved so that the nation would not be devoured by its children. Revolutions, nevertheless, appeared as inevitable, and in the horizon rose those "fearful social and political problems whose resolution is accelerated by the fast development of ideas and interests" (1050). Social and political tensions fed the eruption of fractures within the bourgeois epistemology embraced by Bécquer. His articles acknowledged them openly; his legends and tales articulated them artistically.

Without any doubt, when Bécquer reached maturity, Spain was undergoing a turbulent period. For Rubén Benítez, the 1854 revolution was the most significant event for the writers of that generation. The Madrid barricades frightened the bourgeoisie, conservatives and liberals alike: "Once again, the specter of the French Revolution passes through Spain" (Benítez, 31). The liberal biennial of 1854–1856, characterized by worker upheavals and peasant revolts, was indeed cause for fear.[24] In reality, the twenty years preceding the Restoration of 1874 left

119

a profound imprint on the dominant ideology: 1865 brought the first Spanish congress of workers; 1868, the "Glorious" Revolution; 1871, the Paris Commune; 1873, the First Republic. The revolution "from below" seemed to be taking definite shape. Bécquer approached the revolutionary process with uncertainty and concern. On the one hand, it incarnated a romantic ideal, a manifestation of progress. On the other hand, it carried the danger of going too far. When order became threatened by the action of the "lower" classes, Bécquer immediately distanced himself from the events. In *The Devil's Cross* the popular uprising against the despotic nobleman was portrayed, without any doubt, as justified; and yet it was this specific revolutionary subversion of order that generated the appearance of fantastic beings: a gang of outlaws headed by the specter of the nobleman and "seduced by a future of dissipation, liberty, and abundance" (112) terrorized the region. Banditry and emancipatory insurrections were blended into a single image of terrorific characteristics, following a trend that permeated the majority of the dominant depictions of this social problem.[25]

Revolution, then, appeared both as an inevitable product of economic development and the road to progress, and as a source of tensions and threats to order. This double-bind situation found an artistic resolution in images of the fantastic. Many of the features embodied by the Gothic played an important role in shaping Bécquer's poetics. Marginality, the intrusion of unreason, an ambiguous and paradoxical acknowledgment of social evolution, a fearful approach to revolution, and so on were all elements that shaped a literary production closely linked to the works of a Walpole or a Radcliffe. But Spain in the 1860s, in spite of all the similarities, was not eighteenth-century France or England. Spain entered the age of capital enmeshed in its specific historical circumstances—among which foreign influence and economic dependence figured heavily. Once the new economic organization had been adopted by the ruling classes, the time-gap that separated the Peninsula from other European countries rapidly narrowed.

3

During the second half of the nineteenth century, and in particular during the last twenty-five years, Spain rapidly adjusted to the European configuration—always, it must be stressed, with its own manifestations of "underdevelopment." At the cultural level, Spain's accommodation followed a similar pattern. If Benito Pérez Galdós, who started his production at the beginning of the 1870s, must be equated, as Juan Oleza says, with Balzac and not with Flaubert or Stendhal, a few years later naturalism penetrated the literary circles of the Peninsula almost at the same time that it did in France. By the 1920s, as the examples of Picasso, Buñuel, or the Generation of '27 demonstrate, the artistic panorama of Spain fully coincided with that of the rest of Europe. In fantastic literature, the European paradigm would apply for the period ranging from Bécquer's fearful projections to *The Reason of Unreason* (*La razón de la sinrazón*, 1915), one of Galdós's last works.

Of course, some important differences also emerged. Bécquer might be considered the maximum exponent of a Spanish Gothic, but he incorporated new elements that also linked him to other currents and authors, particularly to Baudelaire. Furthermore, naming a particular production of the mid-nineteenth-century "Gothic" must not, and does not, preclude the existence of other contemporary works that had already attempted to formulate a literature akin to the premises embraced by Hoffmann and Poe.[26] It simply indicates that such a literature fully coincided with a particular social situation in order to formulate a Spanish Gothic expression of the fantastic. It indicates that such an expression became the dominant manifestation of the fantastic, and that Bécquer best represented it.

It is also notable that as soon as the Gothic found a voice in accordance with the Spanish reality, it faded away. The rapid development of social conditions in the Peninsula was in this sense paralleled by the evolution undergone by the fantastic. From *The Shadow* (*La sombra*, 1870) to *The Reason of Unreason* (1915), Benito Pérez Galdós can serve as a clear example with which to frame a literary production that challenged and then denied the foundations of reason that had erected the bourgeois state.

Between the two works (the *Legends* and *The Shadow*), in spite of the two authors' being almost contemporaries, lie profound differences. An obvious but nonetheless significant one is that Galdós's novel takes place in contemporary Madrid. The stories told by Anselmo, one of the central characters, "referred in general to the apparition of some shadow that wandered about in this world with total self-confidence" (4:195). From the start there was no need to summon a distant past in order to introduce the agent of unreason within the framework of representation: the challenge to order erupted in modern society.

The urbanization process, although modest in relative terms, had an immediate impact on the characteristics of Spanish artistic expression. In the popular novel in general, according to Romero Tobar, "urban spaces predominate over rural ones, and, in any case, interior spaces over open ones" (141). Accordingly, as the century advanced, unreason abandoned its marginality and began its move toward the center of bourgeois life. *The Great Miseries* (*Las grandes miserias*, 1876), by García Ladevese, registered the presence of suburbs preying on Madrid. By the turn of the century, the "invasion" would seem complete: "From the outskirts and the slums . . . an evil life penetrates Madrid and reaches the center" (Bernaldo de Quirós, 132). Following the models consecrated by Eugène Sue,[27] the lower classes would be systematically portrayed as barbaric and primitive, and, as Iris Zavala corroborates, the working class would be consistently labeled as "the bearer of evil" (185).

It would be futile to expand on certain characteristics that have already been presented in the treatment of the general European production. The important point is that Spain reproduced a similar pattern: unreason left its limits of confinement to spread amidst the signs of reason, and the ruins of castles and monasteries metamorphosed into the bourgeois streets and houses of nineteenth-century Madrid.

Such a process of internalization found in the house an adequate space of representation. Not only did it serve as a means of registering the advance of unreason, but it also functioned as a symbol both for the bourgeois individual and for bourgeois order. In *The Fall of the House of Usher*, Poe established a clear identification between the mansion and Usher. In *The Shadow*, as Germán Gullón noted, Galdós proposed a similar equation, and he "identifies houses with their inhabitants accommodating space and character" (104). The long description of Dr. Anselmo's "palace" sketches out his own psychological profile: "My house was built very mysteriously; the exterior did not offer anything noteworthy, since it was only one of those old big houses from the last century that still remained in Madrid. In the interior were all its marvels" (4:198). The doctor is depicted as possessing similar traits: his appearance "is not very romantic," for he looks "too contemporary"; on the other hand, he possesses an "extraordinary" personality "alien to present day society." If the inside of the house forms a collection of bizarre and incoherent objects, Dr. Anselmo likewise has an "erudition acquired through assiduous readings that resembled those archives where everything is in disarray, without rhyme or reason" (4:196).[28] Thus, in spite of what might be indicated by appearances, unreason dwelled inside, formed part of the defining elements of the subject. "I am a double being," says Dr. Anselmo, "I have somebody else inside of me, somebody else who follows me everywhere" (4:196). It was, then, *within* the individual that unreason could be located.

Just as *The Fall of the House of Usher* or *The Red Death* imaged the uselessness of protecting order from the invasion of unreason, the house in Galdós could not serve as a safeguard against the tensions present in society. A painting alluding to the Trojan Wars would become the vehicle through which the defining parameters of reality could be questioned: "I always thought there was something 'alive' in that figure [Paris] that, by some unexplained illusion, seemed to move and laugh" (4:201). Paris eventually transgressed the limits of the painting to become a flesh-and-blood character who would seduce the "wife" of the household. The assault on the household became, therefore, a direct attack on marriage, the essence of the family institution.

Seduction and adultery constituted a recurrent theme in nineteenth-century literature. Obviously, such a subject was as old as literature itself. But in the nineteenth century it articulated concrete social problems that would find a particular expression in the pages of fantastic narrative. As Tony Tanner indicates, "it is possible to identify a recurring opposition or alternation of realms in the novel of adultery for which 'the city' and 'the field' provide generic equivalents. This simple distinction suggests that there is an area that is inside society and one that is outside, where the socially displaced individual or couple may attempt to find or practice a greater freedom. Whether there is a genuine outside becomes a problem in the nineteenth century" (23). The fantastic was thus especially appropriate to the issue since it shared some basic thematic elements with the novel of adultery: oppositional realms corresponding to distinct economic organizations whose frontiers become blurred, and transgression of order.

In Spain the artistic representation of seduction and adultery was offered almost out of proportion as the incarnation of absolute unreasonableness. Already in one of Pérez Zaragoza's "galleries" Dompareli Bocanegra, an outlaw with definite vampirelike traits,[29] was presented as the epitomy of evil. After describing all the "horrible machinations" and all the "evil plots" that a criminal could conceive, Zaragoza clarified which one was the greatest atrocity: "At those same hours . . . (should I say it or must I remain silent? Ah! Why doesn't a divine thunderbolt eliminate such a monster from the earth?) At those same hours the vile adulterer safely enters his friend's nuptial bed; and the despicable wife meditates in silence about the possibility of using poison [against her husband], and thus she

124

foolishly laughs at God and at men" (99–100). In *The Shadow*, Paris, although recognizing that he formed part of a long tradition that went back to the origins of Western civilization—the seduction of Helen—introduced himself as a distinct character: "My age is that of humanity, and I have traveled through all the countries of the world where men have instituted a society, a family, a tribe" (4:206). And yet he must not be mistaken for a "falsification of me that wanders about, a certain Don Juan who is an insolent usurper and, at that, a not-too-frightening plague" (4:208). Paris's efforts to distance himself from one of Spain's most renowned cultural myths was not due to "literary jealousy," nor to arbitrariness. On the contrary, in spite of his old age, Paris was clearly the product of modern times: "I [Paris] am what you fear, what you think. That fixed idea that you have in your mind, it's me. . . . In every religion there is a little decree against me, especially in yours that reserves for me the entire last commandment. . . . The big population centers are my preferred residence, for you must know that I find the fields, the villages, and the hamlets unpleasant, and only from time to time do I bother to visit them for sheer curiosity. It is in capitals where I like to live" (4:207). With this statement (which must be read in light of Tanner's words) Paris established a radical differentiation between himself and Don Juan: while he belonged to an urban society, Don Juan was implicitly relegated to a rural world. If the former was the product of the modern way of life, if he formed part of the new mentality, the latter adhered to the principles and characteristics of prebourgeois society.

Two completely different dominant epistemologies sustained José Zorrilla's *Don Juan Tenorio* (1844) and Galdós's *The Shadow*. Zorrilla's "romantic" Don Juan did indeed assume a very different kind of monstrosity. Written at a time when the bourgeoisie was still struggling to impose its worldview, the play's *dominant* perspective still articulated the "unreasonable" premises of prebourgeois society. Don Juan acted precisely as the bearer of reason. He represented the intrusion of the "reasonable" values of capitalism within the spiritual and organic realm of "feudalism": his relations with women consisted of cold-blooded transactions; his conduct was determined by a calculating and dehumanized character; his actions always followed an impeccable logic deprived of any emotion. Hence his monstrosity. Paris, on the other hand, was presented with features more appropriate to an aristocratic gentleman than to a hard-working bourgeois. Hence his monstrosity. He burst into the city, and the house, armed with the tools of unreason: "Oh! I have always loved these places [cities] where comfort, a refined culture, and an elegant idleness provide me with invincible weapons and very efficient means" (4:207).

The different layers—the individual, the family, the house—that unreason penetrated undoubtedly expressed, in condensed form, a more global concern with the contradictions and challenges arising from within bourgeois society. José Selgas y Carrasco clearly attached to the house a symbolic value: "Among the details of the decoration, if they did not represent strictly three orders of architecture they at least represented three orders of hierarchy, three orders of ideas, three ages: the fortress, the palace, and the house; the warrior, the gentleman, and the merchant; the sword, the intrigue, and business; the age of blows, the age of courtesies, and the age of percentages" (139–40). The assault on the house was, therefore, an attack on capitalism. It could come from above, as implied by the representational values of Paris; or it could come from below, as Galdós's *The Golden Fountain* (*La fontana de oro*, 1870) suggested.[30]

Everything that rested outside the domain of dominant ideology ultimately conformed to a single unreasonable and menacing category, a category that would highlight certain characteristics according to the specific social conditions of different historical moments. In 1855 Ochoa associated the guerrilla-bandit, in *Laureano*, with the revolutionary, the artist, and the monster: "Like his republican mane, his Byronian carelessness, and his Satanic smile, he was all affectation, farse, lies" (Zavala,

132). A few years later, Fernández y González would distinguish, in *The Lost Children* (*Los hijos perdidos*), between the hard-working lower class and "the horde of dropouts, the mob that forms barricades, a group formed by whores, card-sharpers, gamblers, beggars, orphans, etc." (85). By 1901, Bernaldo de Quirós would affirm that "the aristocratic scoundrel, the bourgeois scoundrel, the variety of these scoundrels among which must be considered the writer and the artist, are all real shrunkheads or, in other words, useless or unusable elements of the social organism" (21). All the nonproductive sectors of society were thus condemned and engulfed in one single association. But if these elements of bourgeois otherness formed the pool from which to draw an imagery of fantastic tensions, as the century advanced, unreason was to be assigned ultimately to the ranks of the popular classes that threatened the supremacy of the new society. As Iris Zavala indicates, "communism, socialism, anarchism appear at the theoretical level as the destructive agents of the family" (185).[31] Evil resided in the working-class parties, but these were just an extension of a broader sector of the population and, therefore, the characterization could be applied to the popular classes as a whole: "The soul of the people that embrace an evil way of life is, to summarize, the popular soul" (Bernaldo de Quirós, 56). The identification between dangerous classes and laboring classes was thus completed. The claims defended by the workers, even if asserted under the principles of reason, had to be dismissed and, if necessary, crushed. The revolutionary ideal stopped with the bourgeoisie's own access to power, for if carried on indefinitely it would lead to the triumph of "the fourth estate" (the workers) and, ultimately, of "the fifth estate" (the parasitic scoundrels) (Bernaldo de Quirós, 24–25).

Thus the fear of the future was closely linked to class struggle. At the turn of the twentieth century, the conservative Antonio Maura spelled out the conditions and limitations that the ruling class had to impose on its own ideological premises: "To me, the substantive revolution, that is, the transformation of the spirit, the body, and the life of a nation, must always be undertaken from within and from above; it is thus important not to confuse it with what we call revolution from below or revolution of the streets" (Blanco et al., 2:178). When unreason had abandoned its marginal position and begun its inevitable trespassing of the borders of "civilization," the house had appeared in the pages of fantastic literature as the symbolic entity through which the "rape" of order could best be represented. But it was not, by any means, the only conflictive territory. The street, as Maura indicated, likewise assumed a predominant role in the construction of horrific settings. If the house articulated transgression and internalization, the urban streets of nineteenth-century Spain constituted the battlefield on which revolutions and crime engaged the forces of reason.

In 1881 Pedro Antonio de Alarcón wrote *The Tall Woman* (*La mujer alta*).[32] The main character, the engineer Telesforo, is the absolute personification of the modern man who has eradicated superstitious beliefs from his character. However, in spite of his rational and positivist thinking,[33] Telesforo suffers from an absolutely unreasonable fear: "Ever since my infant years there was nothing that could cause me so much horror and fear, whether in imagination or in reality, than a lonely woman, in the streets, late at night . . . I have never been a coward. I fought a duel . . . and soon after graduating from the School of Engineering, I fought and battled against my revolted workers in Despeñaperros, until I reduced them to obedience" (1068). For Telesforo, the threat of unreason resided in the street. It was a threat that could find concrete realization in a series of associated misfortunes: "I could not separate from my mind three different and, apparently, heterogeneous ideas that kept shaping a monstrous and dreadful group: my losses at gambling, the encounter with the tall woman, and the death of my honest father" (1072). Thus, once again, unreason covered the entire spectrum of disruptions of orderly life. What could otherwise be considered a series of coincidences must be perceived as intentionally provoked, since the repetition of misfortunes always concurred with the apparition of the tall woman. She was, in effect, the agent or, more precisely, the cause of Telesforo's tragedies. She was, without any doubt, the monster through which the unreasonable forces of society destroyed his promising life. Not even his house—although "that irrational fear always dissipated as soon as I reached home" (1068)—could ultimately protect him, and he would finally die after a third encounter.

The woman's monstrosity did not derive from any extraordinary or easily recognizable feature. On the contrary, her appearance was said to be typical of any "woman from the common people" (1076). However, something eerie could be objectively identified: "The first thing that struck me in what I shall call *woman* was her very high stature and the width of her scrawny shoulders; next, it was the roundness and fixation of her withered owl-like eyes, the enormity of her salient nose . . . and finally, her young girl's dress from Avapiés. . . . [Nothing could be more ridiculous and terrible than] the effect produced by the bright percale scarf that adorned her face compared with her spur-like, aquiline, masculine nose, that made me think for a moment. . . that she was a man in disguise" (1069–70). Like Frankenstein's creature or Mr. Hyde, the tall woman's monstrosity resided in her deformity, in her admixture of "normal" male and female features.

From marginality to distortion:[34] once the social and economic development had reached European standards, the Spanish fantastic reproduced similar patterns. A few years later, in *Absolution* (*Eximente*), Emilia Pardo Bazán would complete the paradigm: unreason would not need to adopt a shape, and its presence would be acknowledged precisely as an absence, as a void.[35] For by that time unreason had completed its invasion of the houses and streets of the urban world of the bourgeoisie. By that time monstrosity did not require a special form, since it could take any form. Bernaldo de Quirós affirmed that "the people of evil life transform themselves and acquire the aspect, the manners, the representation of the normal population to the extreme that a simple external inspection is not sufficient to recognize them" (132).

In 1915 Benito Pérez Galdós published *The Reason of Unreason*. The title itself is already indicative of the problem addressed by Galdós. The story is in many respects allegorical, and the appearance of supernatural beings is not the primary reason for its consideration within the fantastic genre. On the contrary, as is also the case with *The Enchanted Knight* (*El caballero encantado*, 1909), many of the allegorical aspects of the work are, from a strictly fantastic perspective, counterproductive. It is in the basic premises that sustain it where Galdós fully articulates a fantastic narrative. In the novel, the urban world of Farsalia-Nova is about to expire in an apocalyptic devastation produced by a mysterious force originating from Mars. But, as one of the characters says, the real source of the destruction is not located outside society: "What comes from [Mars] is not wrath, but a powerful wave generated here in Farsalia-Nova by the ethical disorganization which is the foundation of our power. That wave is like a carnival commotion that brings us taunting disguised as logic and lying masked as truth" (6:349–50). The categories that contained reason and unreason, separated as distinct and irreconcilable concepts, have changed their defining premises, and therefore have lost all meaning:

> Atenaida: I'll say . . . that I am terrified.
> Alejandro: Terrified . . . of what?
> Atenaida: Of the dreadful credibility of absurd things. (6:359)

By the turn of the twentieth century, unreason had finally overtaken reason as the dominant epistemology.

4

The preamble to the Royal Order of July 9, 1861, read as follows: "Against the obstinacy with which it is intended to uproot the sentiments of religion and Christian morality, inspiring aversion toward any social category; against the undeclared, insidious, and malevolent war conducted at the shadows of law against law itself, it is necessary to find an efficient defense that can calm down the alarmed spirits and ensure public order by grounding it on reason and justice" (Artola, 177–78). The Order, as Artola indicates, points to the defensive position of a bourgeoisie confronted by the aspirations of the "lower" classes. It was, at the beginning of the sixties, a first contact with organized forces that were using dominant discourse to promote their own social project. These forces challenged law from the shadows of law. But they waged an imprecise war—or so it was perceived at the time. They waged an ideological and material battle against the political forces of reason sheltered by the projected penumbra of that same reason.

Gustavo Adolfo Bécquer was the poet of shadows. Just as the Enlightenment, "the century of lights," revived in its moment of splendor the phantoms of unreason, so did the consolidation of the bourgeoisie in Spain produce its own world of obscurities. Confronted by the society of progress and railroads, Bécquer evoked the signs of confinement: "The Toledo Cathedral. . . . Imagine an incomprehensible chaos of shadows and light, where the colorful rays of the ogives intermingle and fuse with the darkness of the naves, where the lamp's glow struggles and disappears in the obscurity of the sanctuary" (131). Bécquer's world was one of projections in which two epistemological systems joined but each maintained its own identity. Bécquer visualized vague threats arising out of the foundations of the new order, threats that aimed at an uncertain future. As the century advanced, the possibility of concrete historical changes became a social and political reality. The expression of those threats also evolved as they asserted their presence within the realm of representation.

In *The Shadow*, social tensions lost their marginal status to enter fully the pages of the fantastic. The shadow was, after all, the central character. Paris could not be contained within the frame of an artistic spell: he traveled through the entire history of Western civilization to demand a place in the nineteenth-century nuptial bed. Paris, the shadow,[36] emerged within the bourgeois house to engage in a direct assault on the family.

Bécquer acknowledged the presence of shadows. In Galdós the apparition of Paris immediately invoked a questioning of epistemological principles: was he or was he not real? If Bécquer sketched the outlines of doubt, "that sinister spirit of the nineteenth century," Galdós drew a more transcendental problem. Reality, as defined by the bourgeois premises erected during the Enlightenment, was in crisis: "Before I had doubted whether the figure of Paris was real or only a creation of my mind, produced by incomprehensible phenomena; this doubt tormented me. Now, according to my father-in-law, Paris was a real person known to everybody" (4:219). Either Anselmo was crazy or reality obeyed different laws from those proposed by the dominant worldview. The first proposition seems to be the one accepted by the novel; everything, we are told, has a psychological explanation. But, as affirmed by Germán Gullón, in spite of this resolution, the enigma persists (96), for it is not clear whether Paris returned to the painting.

The uncertainty about the validity of the guiding principles of the dominant class reached all fields of social activity. Even science, that great bastion of rational thinking, was endorsed and appropriated by working-class ideology. This appropriation cast a shadow over science's effectiveness and validity. For the socialist Jaime Vera, for instance, science was considered to be, by definition, profoundly revolutionary. The omnipotent role played by science began to decline: "We live—says Pardo Bazán—in mystery. Mystery is birth, mystery is life, mystery is death. And the world! It is a great mystery! We walk amidst shadows, and the guide we have . . . is a blind guide: faith. Science is admirable, but limited, and maybe it will never penetrate to the bottom of things" (1460).

From Bécquer's marginal shadows to a darkness that envelops the postulates of reference: How, then, to discern the contours of reality? The pages of fantastic literature began to address problems of representation, of "reflection": "Luxury [highlighted] the magic with which the glass painted the contours of his figure. In one of these contemplations he saw passing behind his image a shadow that darkened the brightness of the mirror" (Selgas, 26). How, then, to conceive reality? How to localize the source of those shadows?

Bécquer, Galdós, and Alarcón would all assign a form to the image of unreason. Projections into the past or mechanisms of distortion served to depict the profile of monstrosity. By the beginning of the twentieth century, the problems of representation would be more severe. In *Absolution* (*Absolución*) Pardo Bazán alluded to the new dimensions affecting social thought: "I don't see any cause, I don't see a definite origin" (1330), said Federico Molina in relation to the torments that fell upon him. Dominant ideology assumed the impossibility of assigning a face to unreason. Insofar as unreason had been ascribed to the working class, and insofar as the working class was an indispensable component and a necessary product of capitalist society, which challenged it using the discourse of reason, unreason could only be located in capitalism itself, in "the self." From that moment, the preservation of order had to be based on a defense of "the reason of unreason." At that moment, the fantastic began to break its generic chains to contaminate artistic expression at large, promoting this ultimate paradox through the breakdown of all major nineteenth-century bourgeois codes of representation.

The process of internalizing unreason in Spain followed, then, a trajectory similar to that in the rest of Europe—once, of course, the time-gap had been at least partially breached. After the first phase of contact had been established, unreason was quickly accepted as a defining part of the subject. In *The Shadow*, even though Paris and Anselmo were clearly linked— "You gave me life; I am your deed"—they still stood, side by side, as different beings. With Pardo Bazán, internalization went further: "You don't know death, and you yourselves are

133

your own death" (143). In *Absolution* Federico traveled around the world escaping from a vague but pressing menace, looking for a location where he could be free from the threat of unreason. The search was futile. He hid in a quiet neighborhood, locked himself up in his room, set a protective gun on his table—to no avail. He was afraid: "Why, in the middle of my reading, do I remain with my book open, my eyes fixed on a point in space, my hands frozen, my hair electrified over my temples, my diaphragm contracted?" (1331) Federico would eventually commit suicide, as did Juan Enrique Halderg in a similar story, *The Other* (*El otro*, 1910) by Eduardo Zamacois, in the last feasible act he could undertake in order to liberate himself of that "other" that followed him everywhere. "I need to be free so I can kill myself," says Enrique. Such was the final recourse embraced by a bourgeoisie sieged by specters making claims to the future.

By the turn of the twentieth century, reason had lost its status as a fixed concept in bourgeois ideology and epistemology. It therefore had lost all meaning: "Good and evil are relative concepts. I sustain that evil produces good, and vice versa" (Galdós 1960, 6:357). Endorsed by the working-class ideologies, unrecognizable and useless as a tool for affirming bourgeois hegemony, the "reason of unreason" became the last recourse with which to defend the status quo. For the fascist Ledesma Ramos, "the classical phrase that man is a rational being can and must be replaced by the more authentic one that he is a metaphysical animal" (Pastor, 72). The first half of the twentieth century saw the tragic week of 1909, the Soviet Revolution of 1917, the Primo de Rivera coup of 1923, the depression of 1929, the repression of 1934, and the democratic victory of the Popular Front in 1936. Indeed, the dominance of bourgeois reason appeared to be not only darkened by the shadows of historical development, but totally eclipsed by them.

In 1931 Wenceslao Fernández Flores published *Darkness* (*Tinieblas*). One morning, the magistrate Don Jacobo Sanz wakes up to realize that there is no light. The sun does not shine, fires burn without illuminating, lamps do not glow. The entire world is submerged in shadows, in a total eclipse. A fire breaks out, people flee, but there is no refuge, there is no salvation. All is confusion, chaos, anarchy, and the city is finally devastated by the flames:

> But he saw nothing, knew nothing. He stood amidst an incredible darkness, terrorized by the idea of death, of dying at the hands of such an intolerable death, a death that didn't even show its face. . . .
>
> He ran . . . turned around . . . ran again . . . fell. Everything black. The air and he himself were already in flames.

||| SIX |||

Epilogue:
Saturn Devouring
His Children

ONE OF Goya's secret black paintings completed in his Quinta del Sordo is entitled *Saturn Devouring His Children*. Over a dark background, a giant figure, strongly suggestive of the image of a madman, has just bitten off part of a human figure that he holds in his hands. Nothing in the painting alludes to a context or suggests any immediate commentaries about social reality. The horror of Saturn's insane eyes, piercing through the blackness that surrounds them, is conveyed directly to the spectator. There is no visual escape from the horror: no landscape, no symbols of Greek mythology, no objects, no clothes. It is pure horror facing us from the depths of darkness.

Goya's inspiration for this painting might have come from Vergniaud's speech to the Assembly in Paris in 1793: "So, Citizens, we had reason to fear that the Revolution, like Saturn devouring all his children, one after the other, might give rise finally to despotism with the calamities that go with it" (Paulson, 24). If this is the case, then Goya was not commenting upon the atrocities carried out by the revolutionary forces against the symbols and defendants of the ancien régime, against their predecessors in history. On the contrary, the painting referred to the future of civilization. Goya's project, nonetheless, did not become in Spain the example of a social preoccupation fully shared and developed by other writers and artists. The Enlightenment failed to consolidate its agenda, and specific historical circumstances, such as the Napoleonic invasion and the loss of the colonies, would delay for another fifty years the blossoming of a Spanish fantastic.

From 1816 on, the concept that "revolutions constitute necessary, organic components of evolution" became an intrinsic part of the dominant ideology. With it arose a vision that the road of humanity, of bourgeois civilization, of reason, constituted a constant dynamic process that generated its own negation. Saturn is the god that brings civilization; associated with Chronos, he incorporates the notion of time as an agent of destruction. He thus became, at the end of the eighteenth century, a symbol of historical process. Faced with the fear that the creatures he had engendered would rebel against him, Saturn destroyed them. He thus metamorphosed from creator into destroyer, killing his own "self" and ending his own continuity.

The dream of reason produces monsters: the offspring of the Enlightenment threatened from within to terminate the order the bourgeois revolution had instituted in the name of progress. Civilization devours its own propositions. The new epistemology that had tried to exclude unreason from its universe found itself instead defining boundaries, modifying its own premises in order to constantly relocate its margins. At the end of this process, reason would lose its exclusive space, invaded by unreason—in fact, replaced by unreason as the defining epistemology.

In his analysis of Emily Brontë's *Wuthering Heights* Georges Bataille affirms:

> Even though [Catherine Earnshaw] knows that evil resides in him [Heathcliff], ultimately she loves him to the extreme of saying the decisive sentence: "I am Heathcliff."
>
> In this way, Evil, when considered with sincerity, is not only the dream of evildoers, but is also, somehow, the dream of Good. (26)

And Good, as Bataille goes on to say, must be identified with reason. The internalization effected by Catherine would become the key factor in the development of fantastic literature. In retrospect, this seems to be the underlying force that shaped the course of such development. This is not to say that every single work of the fantastic adheres to it—and it is not the purpose of this study to try to defend such a theory. Undoubtedly, some of the subversive connotations pointed out by Rosemary Jackson can be highlighted, at least in some cases. Potentially, the fantastic could reveal the dark side of dominant culture, thus questioning the artistic and ethical premises of the society that had banished unreason from its horizons; but mimetic discourse could do the same. At the end of the nineteenth and beginning of the twentieth centuries, the denunciation of bourgeois discourse saw the possibility of taking advantage of such potential, a fact that could account for the great number of artists of the left who embraced the fantastic as a viable cultural weapon. Nevertheless, the particular expression that the avant-garde and modernism gave to the fantastic cannot be isolated from a path whose roots lay, precisely, in the formation of the industrial society—which helps explain why the political right also adhered to the principles of the fantastic. Hence, ultimately, the fantastic acquires meaning in its historical trajectory. This does not imply that all production that negates the artistic principles of the nineteenth-century bourgeoisie was, by definition, defending an aesthetic of irrationalism—as social realism would attest. The crisis affecting bourgeois epistemology and language could also be exploited by its opponents. Only through particular analyses can it be determined if a work was ultimately defending reactionary idealism or if, on the contrary, it was denouncing the universalization of bourgeois determination of reality.

The artistic explosion that occurred at the turn of the twentieth century may be seen as inaugurating a different epoch in social and cultural development, although such an assertion would likewise require historical perspective in order to fully assess its significance. But such a time was also the culmination of a period: the seeds of the new economic and social organization that we are now experiencing (from corporativism to informatization, from irrationalism to pragmatism) could probably be traced to the events immediately preceding World War

II. Yet the sowing of these seeds was made possible by a specific historical furrow. In this sense the history of the fantastic must be seen as covering the period between the 1760s and the 1930s, and must be included within the history of irrationalism. The "various stages of irrationalism came about as reactionary answers to problems to do with the class struggle. Thus the content, form, method, tone, etc., of its reaction to progress in society are dictated not by an intrinsic inner dialectic of this kind, but rather by the adversary, by the fighting conditions imposed on the reactionary bourgeoisie" (Lukács 1980, 9–10). Nevertheless, when at the turn of the century the relation of political and social forces appeared to open the possibility for revolutionary change in Europe, the adoption of irrationalism precisely as a means of change cannot be equated with the defense of unreason. The former could provide a space for expanding the horizons of an imposed bourgeois perspective; the latter, as history has demonstrated, worked to preserve the status quo, to protect the existing economic order.

As this study has shown, the fears and uncertainties, the monsters of a material and social reality, were neither existential abstractions nor expressions of some sort of human (psychological) attributes. Or, if they were, they were also much more. As social production, the fantastic articulated apprehensions that were deeply attached to the specific characteristics of capitalist society. The perception of monstrosity had significant correlations with the way in which dominant culture defined and redefined its political and economic supremacy, and depended upon the concrete forms of class struggle. On the one hand, the fantastic "reflected" very real threats; on the other hand, it created a space in which those threats could be transformed into "supernaturalism" and monstrosity, thus helping to reshape the philosophical premises that sustained the fantastic and effectively reorient the course of social evolution. It might have been a small contribution within the complex panorama of the development of History. But it was a contribution nonetheless. After World War II, the international panorama changed drastically. New relations of power, the creation of a hierarchy of first, second, and third worlds, the supremacy of corporations, the existence of a nuclear threat—all would be elements that would contribute to a different social order. The rich production of the fantastic that invades our most recent past thus requires the tracing of another history.

In 1792, the artist leaning on his desk dreamed of monsters. Over a hundred years later, the artist woke up to find that he was no longer an artist but a salesman. Even worse: he himself was a "monstrous vermin," an *ungeheueres Ungeziefer*. He was a being defined through negation: "At the moment of consummation, reason has become irrational and stultified. The theme of this time is self-preservation, while there is no self to preserve" (Horkheimer, 128). When the fantastic expands in modernism it attacks the last refuge of reason: language. The fantastic thus becomes the dominant element of art through representation. It is not a matter of liberating fantasy, of negating the strict rules imposed by neoclassicism. It is a matter of destroying language itself. Once reality had been formalized and declared unreasonable, art could no longer claim the possibility of representation. The last barrier of reason was definitively invaded. The destruction of representation through representation—such will be the new paradox that will haunt the twentieth century. But that, of course, is another story.

‖‖■ NOTES ■‖‖

CHAPTER ONE

1. Sigmund Freud, in his study of the uncanny, also indicates the necessity of differentiating between historical contexts when trying to identify supernatural events: "[Our primitive forefathers] once believed that these possibilities were realities, and were convinced that they actually happened. Nowadays we no longer believe in them, we have *surmounted* these modes of thought" (247).

2. "The idea of supernatural presupposes that of natural. And this word, nature, carries so many meanings, sometimes even contradictory, that some philosophers recommend proscribing its usage" (Vax, 16).

3. It must be noted that Louis Vax too, in spite of his definition, only considers "masterpieces" written since the eighteenth century.

4. At the risk of being redundant, I must emphasize that by consensus I do not mean unanimity. Suffice it to glance at the numerous anthologies of the fantastic, for instance, Bernhardt J. Hurwood's *Passport to the Supernatural*, to acknowledge the existence of dissent among critics and scholars. Even within the parameters of this study, works such as Smollet's *Adventures of Ferdinand, Count Fanthom*, published a decade before *Otranto*, could in all probability be considered. As in many other instances in the present book, dates are offered as representative symbols, and not as absolute moments in historical development.

5. I am conscious that, at this stage, extending the Gothic remarks to fantastic literature in general may seem questionable. Nevertheless, the aim of this study is precisely to show that Gothic literature is only the initial expression of the fantastic.

6. "Allegory is a mode that undergoes many transformations in the course of its history, transformations so radical that they cannot be accounted for solely in literary critical terms. . . . Allegorical writing, like other kinds, changes because the material it seeks to analyse is changed—the world and society or, more precisely, people's knowledge and perception of them" (Clifford, 44).

7. From the beginning, romantic and fantastic were closely associated terms, a fact that has led Tobin Siebers to call his study of fantastic literature *The Romantic Fantastic*. Without any doubt, these two denominations are deeply related, and it could be argued that the fantastic is a special expression of romanticism. If the latter can be understood as an artistic movement that incorporated "irrationalism" in general (feelings, sentiments, and so on) into the formation of a new worldview, then the fantastic can be approached as that specific trend that made "unreason" its central focus. This means, of course, that an exchange and overlapping between the two categories can exist. Nevertheless, the difference between irrationality and unreason is a fundamental one, since the first concept does not necessarily imply the negation of the principles of reason.

8. I am simplifying Todorov's classifications, for he also includes intermediate categories, the fantastic-uncanny and the fantastic-marvelous. See in particular chap. 3, 41–57. Ann Radcliffe's stories would actually be considered fantastic-uncanny. Rosemary Jackson, on the other hand, completely assumes Scott's categories. For her, the three possible kinds of narrative are (1) mimetic (or "realist"), (2) marvelous (outside of our accepted understanding of reality), and (3) fantastic (a mixture of the other two) (32–33).

9. I am referring to the subtitle of her book. Jack Zipes follows a very similar approach in his *Fairy Tales and the Art of Subversion*.

10. I am speaking in general terms, within the broad interpretation of a paradigm—which does not preclude single texts' offering completely different perspectives.

11. Obviously, for a genre to be identified, several texts must first have been produced.

12. Using the idea of freedom as an example, Horkheimer states: "If it is true that we must know what freedom is in order to determine which parties in history have fought for it, it is no less true that we must know the character of these parties in order to determine what freedom is. The answer lies in the concrete outlines of the epochs of history. The definition of freedom is the theory of history, and vice versa" (168).

13. I do not pretend, of course, to have exposed a complete or exhaustive account of the studies on the fantastic. It is only a representative selection, and indeed a partial one, for I have ignored ten-

dencies, such as the thematic, that are ultimately irrelevant to the present study.

CHAPTER TWO

1. Translated into English as *The Proverbs*, a more accurate translation would be "the absurdities."

2. Goya seems to reproduce here the theories of Ludwig Heinrich von Jakob, who in 1791 defended the idea that art was a combination of reason and imagination. See, for instance, Béguin, 30.

3. This does not necessarily imply that Cervantes rejects all medieval values. On the contrary, some of the ideals of justice, for instance, are portrayed positively. However, the overall feudal worldview is definitely discarded.

4. "Jacques François Guillauté's reforms face . . . a good future; even if they are not applied, they indicate what is at stake: to immobilize people in time as well as in space" (Roche, 279).

5. It would be very interesting to study in particular the implications that confinement had for women.

6. See, for instance, the works of Roche, Rudé, or Gwyn Williams. "*La plongée [des écrivains] dans les bas quartiers est de même nature que la traversée des campagnes, le voyage étranger, l'aventure utopique, elle permet de convaincre et d'édifier par la découverte d'un dépaysement. C'est pourquoi les observateurs moraux voient dans les manières nouvelles du peuple la preuve de l'imminence d'une catastrophe . . . et la confirmation de la novicité du spectacle urbain corrupteur. La Révolution génératrice de peur sociale prouvera définitivement une appréhension qui n'est pas isolée dans les années quatre-vingt*" (Roche, 47).

7. Among other things, because there are no reliable statistics. See, for instance, Tobias.

8. There is an entire literary current based on the "banditti," whose study is, of course, of much interest (see, for instance, Brunori). The figures of these declassed rebels also populated the novels and dramas of the nineteenth century, such as *Rockwood* (1834), about Dick Turpin, or *Jack Sheppard* (1839), both by Harrison Ainsworth. A related current, in the United States, would be the Western dime novels. In any case, the entire genre lies beyond the scope of this work.

9. According to Foucault, visiting the lunatic remained, until the

Revolution, one of the "Sunday distractions for the Left Bank bourgeoisie" (1965, 68). In London in 1815, the hospital of Bethlehem still "exhibited lunatics for a penny, every Sunday," attracting 96,000 visits a year. Ultimately, though, this practice would disappear, confirming the previous ideological trend of hiding unreason. See also Foucault's *Discipline and Punish*.

10. Thus when Louis Chevalier studies the French Revolution, he notes that in certain respects it "looks like a settlement of scores between two groups of the population, the old Paris bourgeoisie and *the rest*—those who used to be called savages, barbarians or vagrants" (222; emphasis mine).

11. See, for instance, Roche, 279.

12. The destruction of machines would reach its apogee during the Luddite movement, but as George Rudé says, "an early example was the destruction of Charles Dingley's new mechanical saw-mill in Limehouse in 1768" (136).

13. The Marquis de Sade openly traced the correlation between this "new phantasmagoric" literature and the Revolution: "*Peut-être devrions nous analyser ici ces romans nouveaux dont le sortilège et la fantasmagorie composent à peu près tout le mérite. . . . Convenons . . . que ce genre, quoi qu'on puisse en dire, n'est assurément pas sans mérite; il devenait le fruit indispensable des secousses révolutionnaires dont l'Europe entière se ressentait*" (Baronian, 47). For Richard Astle, the English Gothic was also a response to the Parisian events in spite of the fact that it preceded them (43).

14. According to l'Abbé Grégoire, "in the moral order the king is what the monster is in the physical" (Foucault 1965, 187).

15. By the end of the eighteenth century, dreams are, without any doubt, related to reality. They are not a random phenomenon; on the contrary, they respond directly to stimuli experienced either physically or intellectually. "*L'espèce de nos rêves est toujours déterminée par l'état de notre corps pendant le sommeil, à moins que quelque pensée intéressante dont nous nous sommes occupés pendant la veille, n'ait mis les esprits animaux dans un mouvement voilent, & n'ait causé au sang une agitation considérable, qui approche de la fièvre. . . . J'ai dit, 1. que l'état de notre corps, c'est á dire, les sensations qu'il éprouve, déterminent l'espèce de nos rêves. . . . J'ai dit, 2. qu'au défaut d'une sensation produite par quelque circonstance physique, le rêve pouvoit être déterminé par quelque*

pensée intéressante dont l'âme s'est occupée avec effort" (*Encyclopédie* 36: 679).

16. Needless to say, this is not the place to engage in a discussion about the idea of industrial revolution, "takeoff," and so on, nor about the implications and characteristics that such revolution had in different countries. Whatever the terms of the debate, the consensus among historians seems to be that profound changes in the economic structure of the richest or more "advanced" Western countries took place during the second half of the eighteenth century.

17. This problem of a repressed medieval epistemology resurfacing in the enlightened society seems to shape the defining parameters of the fantastic: it is, as we have seen, the necessary background for Todorov's formulation of his theory of uncertainty; and it is the primary consideration of the psychoanalytic school as well as of Rosemary Jackson's basic assumptions about the silenced other.

CHAPTER THREE

1. See Brion, 115. Sylvia Horwitz proposes a similar interpretation—actually she summarizes Baudelaire—when she affirms that Goya "etched animals that looked diabolically human and men that grimaced like animals. By making both utterly believable, he erased the thin line between the fantastic and the real, between the absurd and the possible" (157).

2. Goya was an *afrancesado*, that is, an admirer and follower of French civilization, of the new vision proposed by *les philosophes*. Napoleon's invasions, inasmuch as they implied the destruction of feudal structures, could, then, be perceived as the dissemination of civilization. As Lukács says, "Napoleon, too, did liquidate, completely or partially, the remnants of feudalism in many of the places [he] conquered, as for example in the Rhineland" (1962, 25).

3. Frankenstein's creature could be read, on many levels, as a Napoleonic figure; Lord Ruthven, the vampire, closely reproduces Lord Byron's physical appearance and personality—as seen by Polidori.

4. Rivière's legal situation was complicated by the fact that at exactly the same time that his case was being judged, another trial was taking place: that of Fieschi and his fellow conspirators in the attempt to assassinate the king on July 28, 1835. The Penal Code of 1835 stated

that "the penalty for a criminal attempt against the life or person of the sovereign is the punishment for parricide" (Foucault 1982, 220). Thus, the two cases became linked, and the decisions taken on Rivière's case had bearings on Fieschi's trial. Rivière's situation, then, really and fully unveiled the political connotations of a monstrous act.

5. According to Tobias, as the nineteenth century advanced, the idea that a separate criminal class existed became ingrained in social perception, a "concept [that] developed gradually after 1815" (53). But, once again, this was an abstraction impossible to sustain in the daily routine of life. In France, where the Revolution had a closer and more vivid impact upon bourgeois imagination, the link between pauperism, laboring classes, and dangerous classes was easily established; in England the association was also made. Not only was it in practical terms impossible to distinguish individual or group classifications (and, after all, who could guarantee that today's worker would not be tomorrow's unemployed and the next day's robber?) but, theoretically, there was even an acceptance of proximity, and causality, between poverty and social or political attacks on society. The English dangerous classes "were the 'virus of a moral poison' that threatened to contaminate those around them. Unfortunately, those most exposed to that virus and most vulnerable to it were . . . the working classes, the laboring poor" (Himmelfarb, 397). So even if, as Henry Mayhew put it in his midcentury study of the London laborer and the London poor, the predatory class was the nonworking class, in reality the two were impossible to "separate," since they coexisted in the same social space. Furthermore, the laboring classes could not be totally exempt from the idea of threat since they ultimately represented a political danger, a potential if not actual revolutionary peril.

6. See, for instance, Peithman, 60.

7. In London alone numerous books on this subject were published following the success of Mayhew's articles on the London poor: Thomas Beames, *The Rookeries of London* (1850); C. M. Smith, *Curiosities of London Life* (1853); John Garwood, *The Million Peopled City: Or, One-Half of the People of London Made Known to the Other Half* (1853); George Godwin, *London's Shadows* (1854); Watts Phillips, *The Wild Tribes of London* (1855); and so on.

8. At the same time, of course, Saint-Marc Girardin was constructing a new metaphor in which the manufacturer, as the representation

of civilization, was entitled to suppress as well as oppress those hordes of "barbarians" in an act of self-defense.

9. Of course, there were numerous other reasons for the urban reformations, one of which was the need for wide avenues in order to facilitate the fast deployment of troops into the city—a lesson learned in 1848.

10. Drew, in spite of coming from the American "periphery," shared the values of the British bourgeoisie. The trip to the metropolis offered the possibility of highlighting all those aspects of material and social life that a provincial but aspiring city such as Boston could desire.

11. The opening scene in *The Fall of the House of Usher* immediately creates, as in Drew's account of his descent to the underworld, the proper blurry atmosphere: it is "Fall," at night "fall" and, as the narrator confesses, the situation resembles the "after-dream of the reveller upon opium": "The time of day in Poe's opening is wholly appropriate, for twilight is a symbol of uncertainty and ambivalence. As a threshold symbol, it represents the region between one state and another" (Peithman, 63).

12. In the 1840s, for instance, Max Stirner and Wilheim Weitling were envisioning a future society organized and dominated by the ragged or lumpen classes. This vision could justify, by a demonstration *ab absurdo*, a negation of the workers' demands for more freedom and more control over the means of production.

13. The coexistence of two worlds articulates, as I have been indicating, the presence in society of two classes in open conflict (I am, of course, speaking in very general terms). This dominant trait of Poe's art corresponded, on the one hand, to the general trends present in Western societies; but, on the other hand, it also articulated the specific situation of the American context. There is no doubt that many of the prevalent economic and political currents affecting the industrialized countries of Europe were likewise present in the United States. Thus, for instance, as Hobsbawm indicates, the Andrew Jackson "phenomenon" should be included, together with the English Reform Act of 1832, in the generalized turmoil of the thirties. But other factors modified the American reality in very specific ways. First of all, Europe—in particular London and Paris—was still considered, of course, the great metropolis, the center of bourgeois culture. In spite

of sharing the same values, the New World bourgeois maintained, as William Drew shows in his descriptions, a certain provincial allure. His focus on reality, therefore, originated from a different angle: adhering to the principles of reason, his universe resided on the margins. In America, civilization was literally in barbarity, among Cooper's savages, and the two worlds kept up an inevitable constant interaction. In addition, Poe lived during the years preceding the Civil War and therefore experienced the tensions and contradictions of a society in which two irreconcilable modes of production coexisted under a single framework of social relations. The resolution would come in the form of a war that, in many respects, Poe had already anticipated in the apocalyptic endings of several of his stories. Philosophical polarization and epistemological uncertainty, then, were two problems particularly relevant in the shaping of Poe's worldview.

14. In *Frankenstein*, Victor deduces without hesitation that the monster is his brother's killer after seeing the creature in the vicinity of the murder: "*He* was the murderer! I could not doubt it. The mere presence of the idea was an irresistible proof of the fact" (73–74). Should it be read as a parody?

15. Poe stated in his theoretical writings that a good short story had to pay extreme attention to all details. And yet in *The Fall of the House of Usher*, for instance, when the narrator sees Usher for the first time he notices that a profound transformation had taken place: "Surely, man had never before so terribly altered, in so brief a period, as had Roderick Usher!" (65). According to a previous reference, the narrator had not seen Usher since his boyhood.

16. Even Dupin himself, a split character who combines "the twin nineteenth-century legends of the scientist and the artist" (Knight, 42)—the rational mind and the eccentric—had also an opposite double in the villain Mr. D.

17. In the same visit, Drew also employed images of the "undead": "We went down [to the basement] with them to see them disposed of for the night. The floor of the room was laid in double tiers of narrow rough board stalls, like uncovered coffins, the feet at both tiers coming together, and the heads slightly raised" (174).

18. Freud could have used this story to illustrate his theory of the uncanny: "A valet, of stealthy step, thence conducted me, in silence, through many dark and intricate passages in my progress to the *studio* of his master. Much that I encountered on the way contributed, I

know not how, to heighten the vague sentiments of which I have already spoken. While the objects around me . . . were but matters to which, or to such as which, I had been accustomed from my infancy—while I hesitated not to acknowledge how familiar was all this—I still wondered to find how unfamiliar were the fancies which ordinary images were stirring up" (Poe, 64).

CHAPTER FOUR

1. "Indeed it was this latter development [the debate about the role of the nonrational] which constituted perhaps the most distinctive feature of philosophical activity in the two or three decades before 1914" (Biddiss, 83).

2. After 1875, the European society began to undergo a series of dramatic transformations in its economic, social, and political organization. The emergence of socialist as well as mass-nationalist (conservative) parties and movements, and of a demagogic antiliberal, antisocialist current, signaled, for Hobsbawm, some important new tendencies that "emerged out of the confused tensions of the new era of economic depression, which almost everywhere became one of social agitation and discontent" (1975, 341).

3. A similar contradiction arises in the detective novel (a genre closely related to the fantastic) of the same period. In Sherlock Holmes stories, for instance, criminals are respectable people gone astray and not the old underworld figures, although these also maintained a presence in the popular imagination. As Stephen Knight affirms, "the physical world in which Holmes operates is basically that of the natural audience of *The Strand Magazine*. . . . But much of real London is omitted. . . . The *real* threat to respectable life posed by the grim areas where the working class and the 'dangerous class' lived is thoroughly subdued" (94).

4. In England, the vituperations against the evil effects of drinking dated back at least to the "gin era" of the mid–eighteenth century. In France, the people of La Commune were insistently qualified as alcoholic. See Tobias, 179–82, and Lidsky, 62.

5. The emergence of the "guilty butler" closely follows the development of the service sector, representing one of the most important economic sectors in advanced industrialism. "In Britain, for example," according to R. M. Hartwell, "numbers of domestic servants in-

creased from 0.6 million in 1801 to 1.3 million in 1851, to 2.2 million in 1901, making domestic service throughout this period one of the largest occupational groups" (383).

6. For Rosemary Jackson, the fantastic is by definition a subversive genre because it questions the dominant parameters for the definition of reality and because it voices what society has suppressed. This affirmation needs to be qualified: the questioning of dominant principles does not necessarily imply a "progessive subversion." As modernism showed, the end of the realistic contract also opened the way for very reactionary interrogations of bourgeois society.

7. Perhaps detective novels should be understood precisely as an articulation of this same situation. After all, the police are normally portrayed as ineffective, and the solution of the crime requires the participation of a somewhat eccentric figure who will bring order back to society.

8. "The dream-life which found its culminating expression in the domestic ritual systematically developed for this purpose, the celebration of Christmas . . . [which] symbolized at one and the same time the cold of the outside world, the warmth of the family circle within, and the contrast between the two" (Hobsbawm 1975, 254).

9. "For Marcel Schwob (1867–1905), all appearances are misleading, and behind beauty stands tarnish. . . . In order to escape there is only one solution: to forever renounce seeing reality" (Baronian, 151).

10. Hobsbawm notes that four elements conspired to change the capitalist economy: (1) new technological era; (2) start of an economy of domestic consumer market; (3) end of liberal economy; and (4) imperialism. All of these elements contributed to the delineation of a very different society at the beginning of the twentieth century, one in which the service sector and the rise of corporations formed the fundamental new bases of economic and social activity. One could probably argue that *Dracula* was a novel articulating the new social relations. Stoker did not introduce an individual heroic figure to fight the forces of evil; on the contrary, in the "age of the masses" the struggle against the vampire would immediately organize itself by adopting a corporate structure: "When we met in Dr. Seward's study two hours after dinner, which had been at 6 o'clock, we unconsciously formed a sort of *board or committee*. . . . He made me sit next to him on his right, and asked me to act as *secretary*. . . . The Professor stood up and, after laying his golden crucifix on the table, held out his hand

150

on either side. . . . We resumed our places, and Dr. Van Helsing went on with a sort of cheerfulness which showed that the serious work had begun. It was to be taken as gravely, and in as *businesslike* a way, as any other transaction of life" (210, 212; emphasis mine).

11. " 'Oh God,' he [Gregor] thought, 'what a grueling job I've picked! Day in, day out—on the road. The upset of doing business is much worse than the actual business in the home office, and, besides, I've got the torture of travelling, worrying about changing trains, eating miserable food at all hours, constantly seeing new faces, no relationships that last or get more intimate. To the devil with it all!' " (Kafka, 4). "Gregor tried to imagine whether something like what had happened to him today could one day happen even to the manager; you really had to grant the possibility" (Kafka, 9–10). The two quotations reveal the formal play in Kafka's *The Metamorphosis*: while ordinary "natural" events, such as those referring to the salesman activity, are presented in horrific terms (grueling, torture, and so on), the "supernatural" transformation is reported as belonging to the domain of the "possible."

CHAPTER FIVE

1. I am not affirming that the bourgeois writers and thinkers of the eighteenth century were antipatriotic, but rather emphasizing the basic traits of a perception that dominated nineteenth-century culture—in particular during the first thirty years.

2. "In the meantime, other important events took place: the revaluation of the Spanish tradition by Germans and British, and the invasion of the peninsula by Napoleon that hurt the pride and independence of the proud country. The first aspect at the cultural level, the second one at the sociopolitical, revived a patriotic spirit opposed to the *afrancesados*" (Navas-Ruiz, 45).

3. The "radical" constitution of 1812 that tried to abolish definitively the feudal society never consolidated its program.

4. The loss of the colonies also occurred precisely at a moment when Europe had begun to look for market expansion.

5. For instance, "El castillo del espectro," *El artista* 1 (1835): 16–19, or "Luisa," *El artista* 2 (1835): 40–45, or the novel *El auto de fe* (1837).

6. I am speaking, of course, in very general terms and do not want to stretch the comparison too far.

7. "Born as a medium for diffusing Enlightened ideals and attitudes in the interstices created by the conflict between the Enlightened despotism of Carlos III and the immovable traditional monarchy, the periodical press was regarded as a crucial instrument in the creation of 'la opinión pública,' that phenomenon of liberal bourgeois society with which the *ilustrados* expected to bring about the regeneration of Spain" (Kirkpatrick, 30).

8. See, for instance, the works of Rubén Benítez or Antonio Risco. The Quintero brothers saw "models of a literary genre hardly cultivated in Spain" (Gallaher, 3).

9. For Baquero Goyanes, the Spanish fantastic tale, which is not clearly defined in his book, was born as an imitation of those written in other countries, and in particular of Hoffmann. He quotes a contemporary critic as saying, in 1839, that these fantastic tales were full of "invention, truth, charm and mystery, and lovers of good literature in our country will find in these stories a totally *new type* of impressions and an *unknown field* of imagination and beauty" (236; emphasis mine).

10. It must be noted that for Zorrilla, as the quotation indicates, one of the necessary conditions for an appropriate fantastic context is a society in which "work," and not "idleness," is a defining characteristic. In other words, the fantastic seems to be perceived as a genre relegated to countries in which the bourgeois ideology of production was consolidated.

11. "The majority of works with a marvelous or fantastic theme that we have been able to locate are dated after 1850" (Risco, 44).

12. There appears to be a growing consensus that Bécquer's legends, in general, must be considered fantastic stories. Joan Estruch has edited a selection of the legends under the title *Relatos de terror y de misterio* (*Tales of Terror and Mystery*), asserting in the introduction that the stories included belong to the fantastic tradition.

13. The Madoz Law of 1857, which culminated the process of disentailment, could be considered the most transcendental step in the road to the consolidation of the bourgeois state. Such an "unreasonable" feature had already been denounced in the eighteenth century by Jovellanos, who, in the name of reason, attacked "the monster of entailment" (Anes, 407).

14. See, for instance, Baquero 1949, 568. For Iris Zavala, the romantic historical novel in Spain represents an opposition to the world

of reason offered by the followers of the Enlightenment. As I have indicated, it should be seen as not so much an opposition as an alternative in the process of creating a bourgeois ideology. Marrast dismisses these same historical novels on the grounds that they represent only bad imitations of French literature. Nevertheless, one would have to ponder the reasons for their success in Spain.

15. As José Montesinos said, "Spanish *costumbrismo* seems born out of a crisis of nationality and the interest of the writers, sentimentally, turns to the past, although the present carries them off" (1980, 32). When examining the general literary panorama, the influence exercised by foreign movements and currents cannot be discarded either. Yet at the same time, the specific cultural needs of Spanish society demanded an expression. The end result was a literature dominated by two complementary tendencies. One was the recall of a past subordinated to the ideological requirements of the present (historical novels, legends, traditions, and so on). The other was the presentation of a society modeled after middle-class values—a static society insofar as values were offered as ahistorical, and yet preparing the grounds for a future of progress: costumbrismo. Juan Ignacio Ferreras calls costumbrismo "materialization of relations in their immobility," "materialization of relations without history" (1973b, 133).

16. In 1837, certain aristocratic privileges disappeared; different disentailment laws culminated, in 1857, with the Madoz Law; in 1856, the law that regulated the *sociedades de crédito* was promulgated, a fact that, according to Miguel Artola, "signals the triumph of the capitalist system" (85).

17. In 1854, the printers in Madrid distributed a leaflet condemning the introduction of machines: "Damned machines, damn inventor and damn the first one who showed the introductory road to Spain. Union, union, down with machines" (Artola, 176). This manifestation was not, as Artola shows, an isolated event.

18. Rafael Llopis acknowledges the correspondence between Bécquer's work and an earlier European production of the fantastic: "Bécquer must be located among the first German romantics and among some British or French cultivators of the 'white tendency'. . . . The chronological gap . . . expresses the difficulties of all kinds that fantastic literature had to overcome to open its way in our country" (100).

19. As Guillermo Carnero indicates, "the Gothic manifests itself

fully and originally with Bécquer, although there might be some prior 'à la Gothic' works" (121).

20. "Spain offers the image of a middle class that advances, with ups and downs, from 1845 to 1875, a middle class whose strongest enemy until little before the Restoration was not the new ascending class but rather the old dominant class" (Blanco 1978, 44).

21. The scattered predecessors of Bécquer in a fantastic tradition also tended to locate their stories in other countries. Italy, Germany, and the Scandinavian countries appear as the most frequent "peripheries." See, for instance, Gallaher.

22. Heine's influence should also be taken into account.

23. In his poetry Bécquer, of course, also addressed this question. In one of his most famous *Rhymes*, number 53, nature offers a cyclical pattern of recurrence (*volverán las oscuras golondrinas . . .*), but those elements that had entered into contact with the realm of "man" would not repeat themselves.

24. As Iris Zavala indicates, it was also during the fifties that stories about criminals began to abound in the press (163).

25. Already in 1831 Agustín Pérez Zaragoza, in his *Galería fúnebre de sombras y espectros ensangrentados*, had called the guerrillas that fought the Napoleonic invasion "monsters."

26. Imitations and "unacknowledged" translations must also be taken into account. Salvador García Castañeda indicates that *Los jóvenes son locos*, by Miguel de los Santos Alvarez, is a story clearly connected with Hoffmann's production. Similar judgments could be passed on Zorrilla's *La Madona de Pablo Rubens* (1837) or Ochoa's *Un caso raro* (1836). For the influence of Hoffmann and Poe see in particular Englekirk, Gallaher, and Schneider.

27. Numerous *Miseries* à la Sue appeared in the major cities of Spain. See, for instance, Romero Tobar.

28. It is worth noting in this regard Hobsbawm's commentaries about the accumulation of objects in bourgeois homes: "The most immediate impression of the bourgeois interior of the mid-century is overcrowding and concealment, a mass of objects, more often than not disguised by drapes, cushions, cloths and wallpapers, and always, whatever their nature, elaborated. . . . This was no doubt a sign of wealth and status. . . . Objects express their cost and, at a time when most domestic ones were still produced largely by manual crafts, elaboration was largely an index of cost together with expensive materials.

Cost also bought comfort, which was therefore visible as well as experienced. Yet objects . . . had value in themselves as expressions of personality, as both the programme and the reality of bourgeois life, even as *transformers* of man. In the home all these were expressed and concentrated. Hence its internal accumulations" (1975, 254). Objects in the bourgeois house were fetishized and therefore participated in an economic system in which relations among people take the form of relations among things. Hence objects in the bourgeois house clashed with their protective environment. It was not, therefore, surprising that unreason would manifest itself within the house precisely through objects. Balzac's *La peau de chagrin* or Pardo Bazán's *El talismán* are clear examples of this tension. Baquero Goyanes reserves an entire chapter for stories dealing with objects, attesting to the importance of the subject. See also Romero Tobar, 145.

29. Stories about vampires definitely alluded to the assault on marriage. Besides numerous translations available in Spain during the second half of the nineteenth century, Spanish writers also dealt with the subject. Of particular interest are Emilia Pardo Bazán's *Vampiro* and Rosalía de Castro's *El último loco*, especially if seen in the light of feminist discourse analysis.

30. For Iris Zavala, Galdós in *La fontana de oro* "for the first time explores the sociopolitical problems of the Peninsula. The work consists of a passionate defense of liberal conservatism; the themes or central characters represent the ideals of the liberal bourgeoisie that supported progress but was against popular revolutions" (181–82). In this sense Galdós seems to be taking Bécquer's premises one step further. Juan Oleza also notes the fearful effects that social chaos, the Paris Commune, the guerrillas, and so on had on Galdós (94–95).

31. The emancipation of women and the liberation of the working class were thus intimately associated. In 1880, the program of the Socialist Party (PSOE) openly affirmed this connection: "The constitution of society [must be] based upon an economic federation, a scientific organization of work, and an integral education for all the individuals of both sexes" (Blanco et al., 2:184). The quotation also illustrates how the rational-scientific discourse was being appropriated by the "unreasonable" classes.

32. It is worth noting that Alarcón's personal evolution in his own fantastic writings follows the paradigm established in these pages. The differences separating *Death's Friend* (*El amigo de la muerte*, 1852)

from *The Tall Woman* are significant. The first story adheres to Gothic characteristics—the action takes place at the beginning of the eighteenth century and involves characters belonging to a feudal society—while the second story is contemporary (1860 and 1875), with the characters embracing positivist and rational principles. It must also be highlighted that the monster, in this last instance, is a woman with the attributes of a man.

33. "By fortune or mishap, I am—let's put it this way—a modern man, not superstitious at all, and as positivist as anybody else—although I include among the positive elements of Nature all the mysterious faculties and emotions of my soul in matters of feelings" (1066).

34. Paris in *The Shadow*, like Polidori's Lord Ruthven, presents a distortion of accepted social behavior.

35. This short story in many respects resembles Maupassant's *Le Horla*. A Maupassantian "inspiration" can also be recognized in another story, *From Outside* (*Desde afuera*). Compare, for instance, the following passage with Maupassant's depiction of fear in *La peur*: "The impression of the supernatural . . . at least for me, acquires many diverse forms. It is not only at the moribund's headrest . . . or in the cave at Lourdes, or in the high seas, where the ineffable touches us with its wings. Sometimes, the impact of a glance, the light of some eyes, or the movement of lips articulating solemn words are sufficient" (1250).

36. In *El audaz*, Galdós also introduced another shadow, although in this case he was referring to Robespierre.

|||| BIBLIOGRAPHY ||||

Actas del Segundo Congreso Internacional de Estudios Galdosianos. Las Palmas: Ediciones del Ecmo. Cabildo Insular de Gran Canaria, 1979.

Aers, David, Jonathan Cook, and David Punter. *Romanticism and Ideology.* London: Routledge and Kegan Paul, 1981.

Alarcón, Pedro Antonio de. *Juicios literarios y artísticos.* Madrid: Imprenta de A. Pérez Dubrull, 1883.

———. *Novelas completas.* Madrid: Aguilar, 1974.

Allardyce, Gilbert, ed. *The Place of Fascism in European History.* Englewood Cliffs, N.J.: Prentice-Hall, 1974.

Amorós, Andrés. *Introducción a la novela contemporánea.* Madrid: Ediciones Cátedra, 1974.

Anes, Gonzalo. *El Antiguo Régimen: los Borbones.* Madrid: Alianza Editorial, 1975.

Arenal, Concepción. *La emancipación de la mujer en España.* Madrid: Ediciones Júcar, 1974.

Ariès, Philippe. *L'enfant et la vie familiale sous l'Ancien Régime.* Paris: Editions du Seuil, 1973.

———. *The Hour of Our Death.* New York: Random House, 1981.

Artola, Miguel. *La burguesía revolucionaria (1808-1874).* Madrid: Alianza Editorial, 1975.

Astle, Richard. "Structures of Ideology in the English Gothic Novel." Ph.D. diss., University of California, San Diego, 1977.

Auerbach, Erich. *Mimesis: The Representation of Reality in Western Literature.* Princeton: Princeton University Press, 1971.

Ayguals de Izco, Wenceslao. *Pobres y ricos o la Bruja de Madrid.* Barcelona: Editorial Taber, 1969.

Balakian, Anna. *El movimiento simbolista.* Madrid: Ediciones Guadarrama, 1969.

Bancquart, M. C. Introduction to *"Le Horla" et autres contes cruels et fantastiques,* by Guy de Maupassant, ed. M. C. Bancquart. Paris: Editions Garnier Frères, 1976.

Baquero Goyanes, Mariano. *El cuento español en el siglo XIX.* Madrid: Consejo Superior de Investigaciones Científicas, 1949.

157

———. *Proceso de la novela actual*. Madrid: Ediciones Rialp, 1963.

Baronian, Jean Baptiste. *Panorama de la littérature fantastique de langue française*. Paris: Editions Stock, 1978.

Bataille, Georges. *La literatura y el Mal*. Madrid: Taurus Ediciones, 1981.

Baudelaire, Charles. *Œuvres complètes*. Vol. 4. Paris: Calmann Levy, 1880.

Becker, Carol. "Edgar Allan Poe: The Madness of the Method." Ph.D. diss., University of California, San Diego, 1975.

Beckford, William. *Vathek*. New York: Dover Publications, 1966.

Bécquer, Gustavo Adolfo. *Obras completas*. Madrid: Aguilar, 1961.

Béguin, Albert. *El alma romántica y el sueño*. Mexico City: Fondo de Cultura Económica, 1954.

Benítez, Rubén. *Bécquer tradicionalista*. Madrid: Editorial Gredos, 1971.

Bergier, J. F. "The Industrial Bourgeoisie and the Rise of the Working Class." In *The Fontana Economic History of Europe*. Vol. 3, *The Industrial Revolution*, ed. Carlo M. Cipolla, 397–451. Glasgow: Williams Collins Sons and Co., 1973.

Bernal, J. D. *Science in History*. London: C. A. Watts and Co., 1957.

Bernaldo de Quirós, C., and José María Llanas Aguilaniedo. *La mala vida en Madrid*. Madrid: B. Rodríguez Serra, 1901.

Biddiss, Michael D. *The Age of the Masses*. New York: Harper and Row, 1977.

Blanco Aguinaga, Carlos. *Juventud del 98*. Barcelona: Editorial Crítica, 1978.

Blanco Aguinaga, Carlos, Julio Rodríguez Puértolas, and Iris Zavala. *Historia de la literatura española*. Madrid: Editorial Castalia, 1979.

Borchardt, Knut. "Germany 1700–1914." In *The Fontana Economic History of Europe*. Vol. 4, *The Emergence of Industrial Societies*, ed. Carlo M. Cipolla, 1:76–160. Glasgow: Williams Collins Sons and Co., 1973.

Bosanquet, Bernard. *Science and Philosophy*. New York: Books for Libraries Press, 1927.

Brion, Marcel. *Art fantastique*. Paris: Editions Albin Michel, 1961.

Brooke-Rose, Christine. *A Rhetoric of the Unreal*. Cambridge: Cambridge University Press, 1981.

Brunori, Vittorio. *Sueños y mitos de la literatura de masas*. Barcelona: Editorial Gustavo Gili, 1980.

Cano, José Luis. *Heterodoxos y prerrománticos*. Madrid: Ediciones Júcar, 1974.

Carnero, Guillermo. *La cara oscura del Siglo de las Luces*. Madrid: Fundación Juan March/Cátedra, 1983.

Casalduero, Joaquín. *Espronceda*. Madrid: Editorial Gredos, 1961.

Castro, Rosalía de. *Obras completas*. Madrid: Aguilar, 1960.

Cervantes, Miguel de. *Don Quixote*. Rev. ed. Trans. John Ormsby; ed. Joseph R. Jones and Kenneth Douglas. New York: W. W. Norton and Co., 1981.

Chevalier, Louis. *Laboring Classes and Dangerous Classes*. New York: Howard Fertig, 1973.

Clifford, Gay. *The Transformations of Allegory*. London and Boston: Routledge and Kegan Paul, 1974.

Costa, Joaquín. *Oligarquía y caciquismo, colectivismo agrario y otros escritos*. Madrid: Alianza Editorial, 1967.

Curtis, George William, ed. *Modern Ghosts*. New York: Harper and Brothers, 1890.

Darnton, Robert. *The Great Cat Massacre*. New York: Vintage Books, 1985.

Deane, Phyllis. "Great Britain." In *The Fontana Economic History of Europe*. Vol. 4, *The Emergence of Industrial Societies*, ed. Carlo M. Cipolla, 1:161–227. Glasgow: Williams Collins Sons and Co., 1973.

De Felice, Renzo. *Interpretations of Fascism*. Cambridge and London: Harvard University Press, 1977.

Díaz Plaja, G., G. Diego, H. Juretschke, E. Lafuente Ferrari, J. Marías, P. Ortiz Armengol, J. Pabón, V. Palacio Atard, J. Simón Díaz, and J. L. Varela. *Estudios románticos*. Valladolid: Casa-Museo de Zorrilla, 1975.

Drew, William A. *Voyage and Visit to London and the Great Exhibition in the Summer of 1851*. Boston: Homan and Manley, 1852.

Encyclopédie, ou Dictionnaire Universel Raisonné des Connoissances Humaines. Yverdon, Switzerland, 1774.

Englekirk, John Eugene. *Edgar Allan Poe in Hispanic Literature*. New York: Instituto de las Españas, 1934.

Estudios sobre Gustavo Adolfo Bécquer. Madrid: Consejo Superior de Investigaciones Científicas, 1972.

Fernández Flores, Wenceslao. *Obras completas*. Madrid: Aguilar, 1964.

Fernández y González, Manuel. *Los hijos perdidos*. Madrid: Manini Hermanos, 1866.

————. *Historia de un hombre contada por su esqueleto*. Madrid: La Novela Ilustrada, n.d.

Ferrán y Fornies, Augusto. *Obras completas*. Madrid: La España Moderna, n.d.

Ferreras, Juan Ignacio. *La novela de ciencia ficción*. Madrid: Siglo XXI de España Editores, 1972.

————. *La novela por entregas 1840–1900*. Madrid: Taurus Ediciones, 1972.

————. *Introducción a una sociología de la novela española del siglo XIX*. Madrid: Editorial Cuadernos para el Diálogo, 1973a.

————. *El triunfo del liberalismo y de la novela histórica (1830–1870)*. Madrid: Taurus Ediciones, 1973b.

————. *Catálogo de novelas y novelistas españoles del siglo XIX*. Madrid: Ediciones Cátedra, 1979.

Fohlen, Claude. "France 1700–1914." In *The Fontana Economic History of Europe*. Vol. 4, *The Emergence of Industrial Societies*, ed. Carlo M. Cipolla, 1:7–75. Glasgow: Williams Collins Sons and Co., 1973.

Foucault, Michel. *Madness and Civilization: A History of Insanity in the Age of Reason*. New York: Random House, 1965.

————. *Discipline and Punish*. New York: Random House, 1979.

————. *This Is Not a Pipe*. Berkeley: University of California Press, 1982.

Foucault, Michel, ed. *I Pierre Rivière, Having Slaughtered My Mother, My Sister and My Brother.* . . . Lincoln and London: University of Nebraska Press, 1982.

Freud, Sigmund. *The Standard Edition of the Complete Psychological Works*. Vol. 17. London: Hogarth Press, 1953.

Galenson, Walter. "The Labour Force and Labour Problems in Europe 1920–1970." In *The Fontana Economic History of Europe*. Vol. 5, *The Twentieth Century*, ed. Carlo M. Cipolla, 1:133–83. Glasgow: Williams Collins Sons and Co., 1976.

Gallaher, Clark. "The Predecessors of Bécquer in the Fantastic Tale." *College Bulletin Southeastern Louisiana College* 6 (1949): 3–31.

García Castañeda, Salvador. *Miguel de los Santos Alvárez (1818–1892): Romanticismo y poesía*. Madrid: Sociedad General Española de Librería, 1979.

García Ladevese, Ernesto. *Las grandes miserias*. Madrid: Imprenta de R. Labajos, 1874.

Gener, Pompeyo. *Literaturas malsanas*. Madrid: Fernando Fe Librero, 1894.

Gershoy, Leo. *The Era of the French Revolution 1789–1799*. Cincinnati and New York: D. Van Nostrand Co. 1957.

Gollwitzer, Heinz. *Europe in the Age of Imperialism 1880–1914*. New York: W. W. Norton and Co., 1979.

González Torres, Rafael A. *Los cuentos de Emilia Pardo Bazán*. Boston: Florentia Publishers, 1977.

Guarner, José Luis, ed. *Antología de la literatura fantástica española*. Barcelona: Editorial Bruguera, 1969.

Guerrero, Teodoro. *Cuentos sociales*. Madrid: Librería de T. Sanchiz, 1876.

Guiomar, Michel. *Principes d'une esthétique de la mort*. Paris: Librairie José Corti, 1967.

Gullón, Germán. *El narrador en la novela del siglo XIX*. Madrid: Taurus Ediciones, 1976.

Gullón, Ricardo. *Galdós, novelista moderno*. Madrid: Editorial Gredos, 1973.

Gutiérrez Abascal, Ricardo. *El mundo histórico y poético de Goya*. Mexico City: La Casa de España en México, 1939.

Hartwell, R. M. "The Service Revolution: The Growth of Services in Modern Economy 1700–1914." In *The Fontana Economic History of Europe*. Vol. 3, *The Industrial Revolution*, ed. Carlo M. Cipolla, 358–96. Glasgow: Williams Collins Sons and Co., 1973.

Hayes, Carlton. *A Generation of Materialism 1871–1900*. New York: Harper and Row, 1963.

Hays, Samuel. *The Response to Industrialism 1885–1914*. Chicago and London: University of Chicago Press, 1957.

Himmelfarb, Gertrude. *The Idea of Poverty: England in the Early Industrial Age*. New York: Vintage Books, 1985.

Hobsbawm, E. J. *Primitive Rebels*. New York and London: W. W. Norton and Co., 1959.

———. *The Age of Revolution 1789–1848*. New York: New American Library, 1962.

———. *Industry and Empire*. New York: Penguin Books, 1969.

———. *The Age of Capital 1848–1875*. New York: New American Library, 1975.

Hoffmann, Charles G. "Innocence and Evil in James' *The Turn of the*

Screw." In *A Casebook on Henry James's* The Turn of the Screw, 2d ed., ed. Gerald Willen, 154–71. New York: Thomas Y. Crowell Co., 1969.

Horkheimer, Max. *The Eclipse of Reason*. New York: Continuum Books/The Seabury Press, 1974.

Horwitz, Sylvia L. *Francisco Goya: Painter of Kings and Demons*. New York: Harper and Row, 1974.

Hoveyda, Fereydoun. *Historia de la novela policiaca*. Madrid: Alianza Editorial, 1967.

Hume, Kathryn. *Fantasy and Mimesis: Responses to Reality in Western Literature*. New York and London: Methuen, 1984.

Hurwood, Bernhardt J. *Pasaporte para lo sobrenatural*. Madrid: Alianza Editorial, 1974.

Ilie, Paul. "Bécquer and the Romantic Grotesque." *PMLA* 83 (May 1968): 312–31.

———. "Concepts of the Grotesque before Goya." *Studies in Eighteenth-Century Culture* 5 (1976): 185–201.

———. "Goya's Teratology and the Critique of Reason," *Eighteenth-Century Studies* 18 (1984): 35–56.

Jackson, Rosemary. *Fantasy, the Literature of Subversion*. London and New York: Methuen, 1981.

James, Henry. *The Turn of the Screw*. In *A Casebook on Henry James's* The Turn of the Screw, 2d ed., ed. Gerald Willen. New York: Thomas Y. Crowell Co., 1969.

Jameson, Fredric. *The Political Unconscious*. Ithaca: Cornell University Press, 1981.

Jones, Alexander E. "Point of View in *The Turn of the Screw*." In *A Casebook on Henry James's* The Turn of the Screw, 2d ed., ed. Gerald Willen, 298–318. New York: Thomas Y. Crowell Co., 1969.

Jutglar, Antoni. *La sociedad española contemporánea*. Madrid: Guadiana de Publicaciones, 1973.

Kafka, Franz. *The Metamorphosis*. New York: Bantam Books, 1981.

Kayser, Wolfgang. *Lo grotesco*. Buenos Aires: Editorial Nova, 1964.

Kirkpatrick, Susan. "The Ideology of Costumbrismo." *Ideologies and Literature* 2 (May-June 1983): 28–44.

Knight, Stephen. *Form and Ideology in Crime Fiction*. Bloomington: Indiana University Press, 1980.

Kurrik, Maire Jaanus. *Literature and Negation*. New York: Columbia University Press, 1979.

Larra, Mariano José de. *Artículos*. Mexico City: Editorial Porrúa, 1968.

Laruccia, Victor Anthony. "Progress, Perrault and Fairy Tales: Ideology and Semiotics." Ph.D. diss., University of California, San Diego, 1975.

Le Bon, Gustave. *The Crowd: A Study in the Popular Mind*. London: T. Fisher Unwin, 1896.

Le Fanu, J. Sheridan. *Green Tea and Other Ghost Stories*. Sauk City, Wis.: Arkham House, 1945.

Lenin, V. I. *El imperialismo y los imperialistas*. Moscow: Editorial Progreso, n.d.

Licht, Fred. Introduction to *Goya in Perspective*, ed. Fred Licht. Englewood Cliffs, N.J.: Prentice-Hall, 1973.

Lidsky, Paul. *Los escritores contra La Comuna*. Mexico City: Siglo XXI Editores, 1971.

Litvak, Lily. *A Dream of Arcadia*. Austin and London: University of Texas Press, 1975.

———. *El cuento anarquista (1890–1911)*. Madrid: Taurus Ediciones, 1982.

Llopis, Rafael. *Esbozo de una historia natural de los cuentos de miedo*. Madrid: Ediciones Júcar, 1974.

Llorens, Vicente. *El romanticismo español*. Madrid: Ediciones Castalia, 1979.

Lloyd, Rosemary. *Baudelaire et Hoffmann: Affinités et influences*. Cambridge: Cambridge University Press, 1979.

Lodge, Oliver. *Science and Human Progress*. New York: George H. Doran Co., 1927.

Lovecraft, H. P. "The Beating of Black Wings: Supernatural Horror in Literature and the Fiction of Edgar Allan Poe." In *Literature of the Occult*, ed. Peter B. Messent, 66–77. Englewood Cliffs, N.J.: Prentice-Hall, 1981.

Lozano, Cristóbal. *Leyendas y tradiciones españolas*. Madrid: Ediciones Ibéricas, n.d.

Lukács, Georg. *The Historical Novel*. London: Merlin Press, 1962.

———. *Marxism and Human Liberation*. New York: Dell Publishing Co., 1973.

———. *The Destruction of Reason*. London: Merlin Press, 1980.

163

———. *Essays on Realism.* Cambridge: MIT Press, 1981.

Lydenberg, John. "The Governess Turns the Screws." In *A Casebook on Henry James's* The Turn of the Screw, 2d ed., ed. Gerald Willen, 273–90. New York: Thomas Y. Crowell Co., 1969.

MacAndrew, Elizabeth. *The Gothic Tradition in Fiction.* New York: Columbia University Press, 1979.

Macherey, Pierre. *A Theory of Literary Production.* London: Routledge and Kegan Paul, 1978.

MacKay, Douglas R., ed. *Trece cuentos de misterio y pavor.* New York: Holt, Rinehart, and Winston, 1974.

MacLeod, Roy, and Kay MacLeod. "The Social Relations of Science and Technology 1914–1939." In *The Fontana Economic History of Europe.* Vol. 5, *The Twentieth Century*, ed. Carlo M. Cipolla, 1:301–63. Glasgow: Williams Collins Sons and Co., 1976.

Macura, Milos. "Population in Europe." In *The Fontana Economic History of Europe.* Vol. 5, *The Twentieth Century*, ed. Carlo M. Cipolla, 1:1–88. Glasgow: Williams Collins Sons and Co., 1976.

Mainer, José-Carlos. *Análisis de una insatisfacción: Las novelas de W. Fernández Flores.* Madrid: Editorial Castalia, 1975.

———. *La Edad de Plata (1902–1939).* Madrid: Ediciones Cátedra, 1981.

Marco, Joaquín. *Literatura popular en España en los siglos XVIII y XIX.* Madrid: Taurus Ediciones, 1977.

Marrast, Robert. *José de Espronceda et son temps.* Fontenay-Le-Comte: Editions Klincksieck, 1974.

Marsaud, Marie-Isoline. "The Notion of the Monster in the Works of de Sade and Flaubert." Ph.D. diss., University of California, San Diego, 1976.

Martínez Cuadrado, Miguel. *La burguesía conservadora (1874–1931).* Madrid: Alianza Editorial, 1974.

Marx, Karl, and Frederick Engels. *Selected Works.* New York: International Publishers, 1968.

Maurice, Jacques, and Carlos Serrano. *J. Costa: Crisis de la Restauración y populismo (1875–1911).* Madrid: Siglo XXI de España Editores, 1977.

Maupassant, Guy de. *"The Horla" and Other Stories.* New York: Alfred A. Knopf, 1925.

———. *"Le Horla" et autres contes cruels et fantastiques.* Paris: Editions Garnier Frères, 1976.

Mayer, Arno J. *The Persistence of the Old Regime*. New York: Pantheon Books, 1981.

Messent, Peter B. Introduction to *Literature of the Occult*, ed. Peter B. Messent, 1–16. Englewood Cliffs, N.J.: Prentice-Hall, 1981.

Montesinos, José F. *Galdós*. Madrid: Editorial Castalia, 1968.

———. *Pedro Antonio de Alarcón*. Madrid: Editorial Castalia, 1977.

———. *Costumbrismo y novela. Ensayo sobre el redescubrimiento de la realidad española*. Madrid: Editorial Castalia, 1980.

Morayta y Sagrario, Miguel. *La Commune de Paris*. Madrid: Imprenta de J. Antonio García, 1872.

Moraze, Charles. *The Triumph of the Middle Classes*. Cleveland and New York: World Publishing Co., 1966.

Moretti, Franco. *Signs Taken for Wonders: Essays in the Sociology of Literary Forms*. London: Verso Editions and NLB, 1983.

Münsterberg, Hugo. *Science and Idealism*. Boston and New York: Houghton Mifflin Co., 1906.

Murray, E. B. *Ann Radcliffe*. New York: Twayne Publishers, 1972.

Nadal, Jordi. "Spain 1830–1914." In *The Fontana Economic History of Europe*. Vol. 4, *The Emergence of Industrial Societies*, ed. Carlo M. Cipolla, 2:532–626. Glasgow: Williams Collins Sons and Co., 1973.

Navas-Ruiz, Ricardo. *El romanticismo español*. Madrid: Ediciones Cátedra, 1982.

Nigro, Kirsten Felicia. "José Donoso and the Grotesque." Ph.D. diss., University of Illinois, Urbana, 1974.

Ochoa, Eugenio de. "Introducción." *El artista* 1 (1835): 2–3.

Oleza, Juan. *La novela del XIX. Del parto a la crisis de una ideología*. Barcelona: Editorial Laia, 1984.

Ollivier, Albert. *La Comuna*. Madrid: Alianza Editorial, 1971.

Pageard, R. "Le germanisme de Bécquer." *Bulletin Hispanique* 56 (1954): 83–109.

Pardo Bazán, Emilia. *Obras completas*. Madrid: Aguilar, 1964.

Pastor, Manuel. *Los orígenes del fascismo en España*. Madrid: Ediciones Júcar, 1975.

Paulson, Ronald. *Representations of Revolution (1789–1820)*. New Haven: Yale University Press, 1983.

Peithman, Stephen. Introduction to *The Annotated Tales of Edgar Allan Poe*, ed. Stephen Peithman. Garden City, N.Y.: Doubleday and Co., 1981.

Pérez Galdós, Benito. *Obras completas*. 6 vols. Madrid: Aguilar, 1960.

———. *El caballero encantado*. Ed. Julio Rodríguez-Puértolas. Madrid: Ediciones Cátedra, 1982.

Pérez Zaragoza, Agustín. *Galería fúnebre de espectros y sombras ensangrentadas*. Madrid: Editora Nacional, 1977.

Perlman, Fredy. *Essay on Commodity Fetishism*. Somerville, Mass.: New England Free Press, 1968.

Pierrot, Jean. *L'imaginaire décadent (1880–1900)*. Paris: Presses universitaires de France, 1977.

Pina, Francisco. *Escritores y pueblo*. Valencia: Cuadernos de Cultura, 1930.

Poe, Edgar Allan. *The Annotated Tales of Edgar Allan Poe*. Ed. Stephen Peithman. Garden City, N.Y.: Doubleday and Co., 1981.

Poggioli, Renato. *The Theory of the Avant-Garde*. Cambridge and London: Harvard University Press, 1968.

Polidori, John. *The Vampyre*. New York: Dover Publications, 1966.

Poovey, Mary. "My Hideous Progeny: Mary Shelley and the Feminization of Romanticism." *PMLA* 95 (1980): 332–47.

Potocki, Jan. *The Saragossa Manuscript*. New York: Orion Press, 1960.

———. *The New Decameron*. New York: Orion Press, 1966.

Poulantzas, Nicos. *Fascisme et dictature*. Paris: François Maspero, 1970.

Rabkin, Eric S. *The Fantastic in Literature*. Princeton: Princeton University Press, 1976.

Radcliffe, Ann. *The Mysteries of Udolpho*. New York: Holt, Rinehart and Winston, 1963.

———. *The Novels*. New York: Georg Olms Verlag Hildesheim, 1974.

Reed, Glenn A. "Another Turn on James' *The Turn of the Screw*." In *A Casebook on Henry James's* The Turn of the Screw, 2d ed., ed. Gerald Willen, 189–99. New York: Thomas Y. Crowell Co., 1969.

Risco, Antonio. *Literatura y fantasía*. Madrid: Taurus Ediciones, 1982.

Robbins, Michael. *The Railway Age in Britain*. Baltimore: Penguin Books, 1965.

Roche, Daniel. *Le peuple de Paris: Essai sur la culture populaire au XVIII siècle*. Paris: Editions Aubier Montaigne, 1981.

Rodríguez Almodóvar, Antonio. *Los cuentos maravillosos españoles*. Barcelona: Editorial Crítica, 1982.

Rodríguez-Puértolas, Julio, ed. *El caballero encantado*, by Benito Pérez Galdós. Madrid: Ediciones Cátedra, 1982.

Rogers, Douglass M., ed. *Benito Pérez Galdós.* Madrid: Taurus Ediciones, 1973.

Romero Tobar, Leonardo. *La novela popular española del siglo XIX.* Madrid: Editorial Ariel, 1976.

Ros de Olano, Antonio. *Cuentos estrambóticos y otros relatos.* Barcelona: Editorial Laia, 1980.

Rowbothan, Sheila. *Hidden from History.* New York: Random House, 1976.

Rubin, Louis D., Jr. "One More Turn of the Screw." In *A Casebook on Henry James's* The Turn of the Screw, 2d ed., ed. Gerald Willen, 350–66. New York: Thomas Y. Crowell Co., 1969.

Rudé, George. *Ideology and Popular Protest.* New York: Pantheon Books, 1980.

Saenz-Alonso, Mercedes. *Don Juan y el donjuanismo.* Madrid: Ediciones Guadarrama, 1969.

Sainz de Robles, Federico Carlos. *La promoción de "El Cuento Semanal" 1907–1925.* Madrid: Espasa-Calpe, 1975.

Samuel, Raphael. *East End Underworld: Chapters in the Life of Arthur Harding.* London, Boston, and Henley: Routledge and Kegan Paul, 1981.

Sauvage, Micheline. *Le cas Don Juan.* Paris: Editions du Seuil, 1953.

Savater, Fernando. *La infancia recuperada.* Madrid: Taurus Ediciones, 1977.

Sayers, Sean. *Reality and Reason: Dialectic and the Theory of Knowledge.* New York and Oxford: Basil Blackwell, 1985.

Scanlon, Geraldine M. *La polémica feminista en la España contemporánea.* Madrid: Siglo XXI de España Editores, 1976.

Schichel, Richard. *The World of Goya 1746–1828.* New York: Time-Life Books, 1967.

Schiller, Daniel. *Objectivity and the News: The Public and the Rise of Commercial Journalism.* Philadelphia: University of Pennsylvania Press, 1981.

Schneider, Franz. "E.T.A. Hoffmann en España: Apuntes bibliográficos e históricos." In *Estudios eruditos in memoriam de Adolfo Bonilla y San Martín.* Madrid: Imprenta Viuda e Hijos de Jaime Rates, 1927.

Sebold, Russell P. *Trayectoria del romanticismo español: Desde la ilustración hasta Bécquer.* Barcelona: Editorial Crítica, 1983.

Selgas y Carrasco, José. *Novelas.* Madrid: Imprenta de A. Pérez Dubrull, 1885.

Shelley, Mary. *Frankenstein, or The Modern Prometheus.* New York: New American Library, 1965.

Siebers, Tobin. *The Romantic Fantastic.* Ithaca and London: Cornell University Press, 1984.

Sobejano, Gonzalo. *Nietzche en España.* Madrid: Editorial Gredos, 1967.

Sontag, Susan. *Illness as Metaphor.* New York: Vintage Books, 1977.

Souviron, José María. *El príncipe de este siglo.* Madrid: Ediciones Cultura Hispánica, 1968.

Steiner, George. *In Bluebeard's Castle; Some Notes towards the Redefinition of Culture.* New Haven: Yale University Press, 1971.

Stevenson, Robert Louis. *The Works of R. L. Stevenson. Vailima Edition.* New York: Charles Scribner's Sons, 1922.

Stoker, Bram. *The Annotated Dracula.* New York: Ballantine Books, 1975.

Street, Brian V. *The Savage in Literature. Representations of "Primitive" Society in English Fiction 1858–1920.* London and Boston: Routledge and Kegan Paul, 1975.

Tanner, Tony. *Adultery in the Novel.* Baltimore and London: The Johns Hopkins University Press, 1979.

Terry, R. C. *Victorian Popular Fiction 1860–1880.* Atlantic Highlands, N.J.: Humanities Press, 1983.

Thompson, G. R. "A Dark Romanticism: In Quest of a Gothic Monomyth." In *Literature of the Occult,* ed. Peter B. Messent, 31–39. Englewood Cliffs, N.J.: Prentice-Hall, 1981.

Tobias, J. J. *Crime and Industrial Society in the 19th Century.* New York: Schocken Books, 1967.

*Todorov, Tzvetan. *The Fantastic.* Ithaca: Cornell University Press, 1973.

Tompkins, J.M.S. *The Popular Novel in England 1770–1800.* Westport, Conn.: Greenwood Press, 1976.

Tuñon de Lara, Manuel. *La España del siglo XIX.* Barcelona: Editorial Laia, 1976.

———. *Estudios sobre el siglo XIX.* Madrid: Siglo XXI de España Editores, 1978.

———. *Medio siglo de cultura española.* Barcelona: Editorial Bruguera, 1982.

Varela Jacomé, Benito. *Estructuras novelísticas del siglo XIX.* Barcelona: Hijos de José Bosch, 1974.

168

Varma, Devendra P. "Quest of the Numinous: The Gothic Flame." In *Literature of the Occult*, ed. Peter B. Messent, 40–50. Englewood Cliffs, N.J.: Prentice-Hall, 1981.

Varnado, S. L. "The Idea of the Numinous in Gothic Literature." In *Literature of the Occult*, ed. Peter B. Messent, 51–56. Englewood Cliffs, N.J.: Prentice-Hall, 1981.

Vax, Louis. *Las obras maestras de la literatura fantástica*. Madrid: Taurus Ediciones, 1981.

Veblen, Thorstein. *The Theory of the Leisure Class*. Boston: Houghton Mifflin Co., 1973.

Villacorta Baños, Francisco. *Burguesía y cultura: Los intelectuales españoles en la sociedad liberal 1808–1931*. Madrid: Siglo XXI de España Editores, 1980.

Vold, George B. "Social-Cultural Conflict and Criminality." In *Crime and Culture*, ed. Marvin E. Wolfgang, 33–41. New York, London, Sidney, and Toronto: John Wiley and Sons, 1968.

Walpole, Horace. *The Castle of Otranto*. New York: Dover Publications, 1966.

Weber, Max. *El político y el científico*. Madrid: Alianza Editorial, 1968.

West, Muriel. "The Death of Miles in *The Turn of the Screw*." In *A Casebook on Henry James's* The Turn of the Screw, 2d ed., ed. Gerald Willen, 338–49. New York: Thomas Y. Crowell Co., 1969.

Wilde, Oscar. *De profundis*. New York: Avon Books, 1964.

Williams, Gwyn A. *Artisans and Sans-Culottes*. New York: W. W. Norton and Co., 1969.

Wilson, Edmund. "The Ambiguity of Henry James." In *A Casebook on Henry James's* The Turn of the Screw, 2d ed., ed. Gerald Willen, 115–53. New York: Thomas Y. Crowell Co., 1969.

Winks, Robin W., ed. *Detective Fiction*. Englewood Cliffs, N.J.: Prentice-Hall, 1980.

Wolfgang, Marvin E., ed. *Crime and Culture*. New York, London, Sidney, and Toronto: John Wiley and Sons, 1968.

Zamacois, Eduardo. *Obras selectas*. Barcelona: Editorial AHR, 1973.

Zavala, Iris M. *Ideología y política en la novela española del siglo XIX*. Salamanca: Ediciones Anaya, 1971.

Zipes, Jack. *Fairy Tales and the Art of Subversion*. New York: Wildman Press, 1983.

Zorrilla, José. *Don Juan Tenorio*. Madrid: Espasa-Calpe, 1975.

‖‖ INDEX ‖‖

171

WIDENER UNIVERSITY
WOLFGRAM
LIBRARY
CHESTER, PA.

DATE DUE

DEC 1 3 2002			

DEMCO 38-297